I0667770

Planet Evë Series

Tessr Games

Derek A Morrison

Planet Evë
Series:

 The
Anient Five

 Tessr
Games

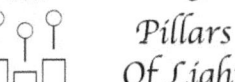 Book Of
Megi

 Pillars
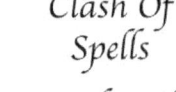 Of Light

Clash Of
Spells

Realm Of
Darkness

 The Ultimate
Plan

 Lance's
War

 The Final
Battle

Derek A Morrison was born and raised in Sidney, Nebraska. After graduating high school in May of 2010, he moved to Colorado where he currently resides with his family. Derek has a strong passion for writing and enjoys every moment of it. He also enjoys watching TV shows, being outside, and spending time with his family. "Always believe in yourself and never give up what drives that belief."

~Derek A Morrison

Table of Contents

Chapter One:

The End Is Only The Beginning

After a few days of rest and recovery, Oshwaia activated four luminätas. With all four lit, there was enough light to cover the labyrinth; destroying every dark creature in its path. After he returned to the temple, Jessica, Father Bria, Father Paul, Drake, and himself cast a spell, creating levels underneath the labyrinth's new "ground" level. The first new level was for housing and living followed by the level for food and water.

The hiumäns explored the labyrinth and the levels. All of the entrances to the labyrinth were sealed shut by Oshwaia and made hidden from those who don't know about them.

"It's perfect!" Kim shouted as she came running out of sector D-1, her new home. Jessica was right behind her.

"I agree!" Jessica said as the two caught up with Drake and Zack.

"That's good to hear," Drake said.

"Where are you staying Drake?" Kim asked.

"Over there," he said as he pointed towards the end of D-2, "down the hallway to E."

"Come on guys. Father Bria, Father Paul, and Oshwaia want to talk to us in C-7." Jessica said as she took off towards the temple. The others were right behind her. Once in C-7, the three were prepared for Drake and his friend's arrival.

"We need to come up with a way to defeat Lord Taoî," Father Paul started off," the three of us were talking and with there being so little Light left in the universe, it's only a matter of time before the barriers are too weak to hold the Darkness out."

"How long do we have?" Jessica asked. Silence filled the room.

"How long?" Drake asked.

"Several years at least," Oshwaia answered.

"Then we need some kind of defense to prepare us," Drake said. Everyone agreed. If Darkness was really coming and no way of stopping it, then the last line of defense was their only option; but how could they defend themselves?

"I wish to speak with Drake alone please," Oshwaia said then left the room. Drake followed him.

"What did you want to talk about?" Drake asked as he hurried to catch up with Oshwaia.

"Come," was all he said as he left C and headed towards the temple. Very confused, Drake still followed him. Once they got to the temple, they climbed upwards. The two journeyed all the way to the very top of the temple. At the top was a small room with a round stone table in the center of it. Engraved in the center of the table was the Tërcerlin symbol.

"Long ago, we used to watch other species battle one another," Oshwaia began as he stared out a hole in the wall overlooking the Labyrinth below, "sometimes for sport, sometimes to kill." An eerie silence quickly covered the room. Oshwaia suddenly continued, "I believe that if we are to have any chance at defeating Lord Taoî and Darkness, we need to battle one another."

"I agree, but how?" Drake asked. Oshwaia turned around.

"Tessrocisy," he paused, "it is an ancient phrase which means 'Rise of Hope'. We have to make sure everyone knows there is still hope."

"What if we held a quest? It could be a series of challenges on different levels that would help prepare one victor per quest to help serve the Light." Drake paused, "We could call it The Tessr Games." There was another brief pause.

"I like it," Oshwaia said in a happy tone, "then I'll personally train each winner the 'Ancient Ways'."

"What are the 'Ancient Ways'?" Drake asked. Oshwaia walked up to Drake, grabbed his hand with the Tërcerlin symbol on it, and placed it directly on top of the Tërcerlin symbol that was on the stone table. First, Drake's symbol started to glow green. Then, the stone symbol started to glow the same green. Oshwaia pulled Drake's hand away and his symbol's glow slowly faded away. The symbol on the stone table shot a laser upward then a grid of lasers appeared above the entire table, not exceeding the end though. Suddenly, five symbols appeared above the grid, circling clockwise.

"Fire, water, earth, air, and, "Drake paused, confused.

"Yes, the Tërcerlin symbol," Oshwaia finished Drake's sentence. He paused a moment, then continued. "After the universe was created, Queen Evë saw us to be the most intelligent species and entrusted us with the four elements of life and the Tërcerlin symbol, made from pure Light. Five of us were chosen to pick an element and study it; learn it. Successfully, one by one, my brothers and I learned to control each element."

"You were chosen? Which one did you choose?" Drake asked excitedly.

"The most powerful one of them all," Oshwaia answered. Drake looked at the symbol on his hand, knowing what Oshwaia meant. "Each element was called an 'Ancient Way'," Oshwaia continued. "When Lord Taoî fired the Murcurî Cannon and when Cruz exploded, I was the only one who survived. I swore upon my life that one day, I would teach someone the 'Ancient Ways'. Now is that time." The two stood there, smiling at each other. Suddenly, all of the lazars disappeared and the symbols faded away.

"I'll go tell the others," Drake happily said, turned around, and started to leave.

"One more thing," Oshwaia said calmly. Drake stopped and went back to Oshwaia.

"Yes?" he asked.

"I have a task that I would like to entrust to you and you alone." Oshwaia answered. Drake looked very confused at this point.

"What's that?" he asked.

"I want you to learn all five 'Ancient Ways'. You have already started mastering the Tërcerlin symbol."

"Sure," Drake interrupted.

"It will be very hard, very painful, and it might even kill you," Oshwaia continued. Drake thought about it. "I will help you," Oshwaia encouraged him. There was a brief pause.

"Let's do it!" Drake said determinedly.

"Our secret," Oshwaia warned.

"Our secret," Drake agreed then ran off to tell the others about their defense plan and to begin the revolution.

Chapter Two:
Five Years Later

The first annual Tessr Games was rough. Only thirty people tried out and there were only five stages. The winner was Caryn Liverpool, winning the Alci Statue. The second annual Tessr Games was a bit better than the first. Fifty people volunteered with two new stages added. The Unratraus Statue was awarded to the winner, Ryan McNalley. Nothing changed about the third annual Tessr Games, fifty people and seven stages. The winner for that year though was Jared Olson, who received the Fuque Statue. The winner of the fourth annual Tessr Games was Tori Eckerburg, who was honored with the Wazi Statue. However, seventy-five people volunteered and two new stages were added that year.

The fifth annual Tessr Games was in for a big surprise. Opening day for the Tessr Games was approaching and news about the games had finally arrived. Door to door, flyers were handed out about the upcoming games:

In three days, in the new Tessr Games Arena, one hundred contestants will battle each other in ten new stages for the grand prize of a rare statue and the honor of training with the last archaic.
Registration starts today at the Labyrinth Arena.

"Thanks again for the flyer Mrs. Eckerburg," Drake said.

"Please, call me Tori," she said then headed off to flyer zone A. Drake examined the flyer. He decided he'd go check out who was registering, after he finished taking a package to Jane Florence in B-2. The package was delivered successfully so

Drake hurried up to the Labyrinth Arena. When he got there, he was amazed at the crowd of people. After a while, the registration list was starting to get full.

"Drake! Drake!" Jessica called out from the crowd at him. She made her way out of the crowd and over to Drake.

"Hey Drake!" she said excitedly.

"Hey Jess, what are you doing here?" Drake asked.

"Registering to compete this year," she said proudly, "what about you? Are you going to register?"

"Me? Oh no!"

"Why not? Look at what you did five years ago. You'd be perfect at this."

"Thanks but I lost five years ago."

"What do you mean?" she asked as the two sat down.

"I had them; all five artifacts," Drake said, sounding depressed.

"You made the right choice Drake. I would've done the same thing."

"Do you really think so?" Drake asked, a bit nervously.

Jessica grabbed one of Drake's hands, "I really do!" It was at that moment that a small spark of love ignited within the two. They slowly started moving in towards each other.

"The registration is about full. I repeat, the registration is about full," yelled Father Brai's voice from the registration table, "last call for registration."

"Last call," Jessica said as she got up, kissed Drake on the cheek, then disappeared off into the crowd. Drake started to daze off because of the kiss.

"The games," came Queen Evë's voice from inside Drake's head, snapping him out of his trance. Drake immediately got up and ran as fast as he could to the registration table, shoving people out of his way.

"Well Drake, I didn't expect to see you here," Father Izea said somewhat rudely. Ever since the two first met, he had never really liked Drake. He always thought Drake was too young for his responsibilities, even five years later.

"Well surprise," Drake responded sarcastically towards him.

"What can we do for you Drake?" Father Paul asked him.

"I would like to register," he answered.

"As a contestant?" Father Izea busted out, shocked beyond belief.

"Yes. As a contestant," Drake said calmly, ignoring his stupidity.

"Are you sure Drake?" Father Brai asked, "It can be very dangerous." Drake looked him dead in the eyes.

"I think I can handle it," Drake said seriously. Father Brai just smiled.

"Then sign here," Father Paul said as he showed Drake where to begin registering. With Drake's signature, they had all one hundred contestants for the fifth annual Tessr Games.

"Ladies and gentlemen," Father Brai shouted as he stood up, "your attention ladies and gentlemen. Congratulations to all of you who have signed up for this year's games. I'm happy to say that all one hundred spots are full this year." Everyone in the crowd clapped and cheered in excitement. "Starting tomorrow morning at the sound of the bells, report back here. Each of you will go through an evaluation test with either myself, Father Paul," who stood up and waved, "or

Father Izea," who also stood up and waved. "Get plenty of rest and see you all tomorrow morning!" Everyone clapped and cheered again. Afterwards, the crowd started to break up.

"Alright, well good night," Drake said.

"Good night," Father Bria and Father Paul responded but Father Izea just rolled his eyes.

The next morning, Drake and Jessica immediately went to Father Brai, Father Paul, and Father Izea, only to find out there was no Father Izea.

"Ah you two, there you are," Father Paul said cheerfully as the two approached the registration table, "there's someone I'd like you to meet."

"I'm Father Mika, it's a pleasure to meet you," the man to the left said as he stood up and shook Drake's hand.

"I'm Drake," he responded, smiling. Then he shook Jessica's hand.

"And I'm Jessica," she said, smiling as well. The two looked around for Father Izea. "Where's Father Izea?" Jessica asked as Father Mika sat down.

"He said he was sick and couldn't make it today," Father Brai answered. Drake thought that was a little strange because as far as he was told, Father Izea never got sick. Father Brai then stood up.

"Ladies and gentlemen," he shouted, "can I have your attention please!" Shortly afterwards, silence fell and all the attention was on Father Brai. "Good morning and thank you for coming. Here shortly, each of you will be split up into three separate groups, and then evaluated individually. When you hear your name called, go to that group leader and the evaluations will begin shortly. But before we begin, please welcome Father Mika, who will be filling in for Father Izea, who is currently ill and could not make it at this time." Father Mika stood up and waved. Everyone clapped to welcome him. "When you hear your name, report to your group leader," he picked up his paper, "Carol Ignita, Daniel Floid," he continued down his list but neither Drake's nor Jessica's name was called. Next was Father Mika's list. He started reading off the names.

"Jessica McGee," he shouted.

"Well that's me," she said smiling at Drake, "good luck."

"Thanks, you too," he replied. Father Mika continued down the list when all of a sudden Drake's name was called. For some odd reason, he felt relieved. Maybe it was because he was in the same group as Jessica. He quickly hurried to the group, looking for his friend. By the time he found Jessica, the last name of the list was called.

"And Lance Jefferson," Father Mika finished, then Father Paul started his list. When Drake heard that name, something inside told him that Lance Jefferson was not to be trusted. Suddenly, Lance was right in front of them.

"Hi, I'm Lance, Lance Jefferson," he said with his hand stuck out and a smile on his face.

"Hi, I'm Jessica McGee," Jessica said as she smiled and shook his hand. Then he turned to Drake. The moment their hands met, that bad feeling got worse.

"Hey, I'm Drake Shaw," he said, shaking his hand but faking the smile.

"Alright. Let the evaluation test begin," shouted Father Brai, and the tests began. Father

Mika started calling the members of his group one by one to a table. Drake was called towards the beginning of the list. When he got to the table, a series of tests and questions were asked; age, height, weight, favorite color, pick a symbol (fire, water, earth, air, or Tёrcerlin), etc. Each answer was written down.

"Why do you collect our answers? What are they for?" Drake asked after the last question.

"I'm not supposed to say," Father Mika said as he looked around to make sure no one was listening/looking, "but here, take this." He secretly handed Drake a small list. It was the order of the stages for this year's games. "Promise me you won't share this with anyone," he asked Drake.

"I promise," he replied. He quickly put the list away.

"Off you go," Father Mika smiled then called the next contestant. After all of the contestants were done with their tests, everyone was allowed to leave until the next day. Drake was one of the last people to leave, but just as he was about to go, he noticed Lance standing in a corner, staring up into the stands. He waited until they were the last two. Just like that, Lance left and Drake followed him, only until he headed towards zone C; his home. Drake just knew something was wrong with Lance; something dark.

The next few days were full of intense training. By the time lunchtime came around, every single contestant was sweating like crazy. After lunch, the training was more intense. Soon, Opening Ceremony came.

Just as the first hiumäns started to wake up on the day of the ceremony, Father Brai, Father Mika, and Father Paul were all together, worrying about Father Izea.

"Has anyone seen Father Izea?" Father Brai finally asked.

"Not since the day of the registration," Father Paul said.

"Yeah, same here," replied Father Brai, "how about you Father Mika?"

"Not since I first met him at the initiation," he answered.

"This is very strange," Father Brai said suspiciously, "I'll go check his place and I'll meet you two later at the Opening Ceremony."

"Right," Father Mika and Father Paul agreed. Father Brai got up and left the Labyrinth Arena. He walked all the way to the temple when off in the distance, he swore he heard a noise, almost like something closing. He stopped and listened but didn't hear anything. He continued on, down towards the housing level. Inside C-7, Father Izea seemed to be the only resident living in that sector. Father Brai searched Father Izea's home from top to bottom but still no sign of Father Izea.

"Where could he be?" Father Brai sat there, wondering where he could possibly be.

"Your attention, can I have everyone's attention please," Oshwaia said into the speaker. The crowd in the arena simmered down. "Thank you," he started off, "and welcome to the fifth annual Tessr Games!" The crowd cheered and hollered for a moment. "This year, we have some exciting new announcements. To begin, please welcome all one hundred contestants." He pointed to all one hundred contestants in the arena below. Like before, the crowd cheered and hollered. The crowd shortly calmed down and Oshwaia continued. "Also, we have changed some levels as well as adding a brand new level, making this year's ten level games the most spectacular year yet!" The crowd almost went insane with excitement. After a few moments, the crowd quieted down. "And now," Oshwaia said, "let the fifth annual Tessr Games be...."

Boom, a loud noise interrupted Oshwaia. *Boom* came the noise again, from above the arena. *Boom* it came again. Instantly, Oshwaia and Drake knew exactly what it was; Darkness was trying to get in.

The ceremony immediately ended and Oshwaia, Drake, Zack, Jessica, Father Brai, Father Mika, and Father Paul followed the consistent *Booming* noise up to the ground level of the Labyrinth; the labyrinth itself. The *Boom* noise led them to the opening at the library in Jewel City. As soon as they got to the sealed opening, the *Boom* noise stopped. Everyone looked around but nothing seemed off or wrong until....

"Hey guys, look" Father Mika shouted. Everyone hurried over to him. He was pointing at a shoe that belonged to Father Izea.

"It's Father Izea's alright," Father Brai said, "but where is he?" *Boom* came the noise again directly above them. As soon as the noise came, Oshwaia fell. Drake and Jessica hurried over to him and helped him back up. Oshwaia looked up, towards the noise. One by one, they were all looking upward.

"The seal has been broken," Oshwaia said slowly yet seriously.

"What?" Everyone else said simultaneously and quickly looked at Oshwaia, who kept looking upward.

"Father Izea," Drake said quietly as he looked back up, "what have you done?"

Chapter Three:
On The Surface

"My lord, the syclore has arrived at the location you requested," Michael Cashner said.

"Excellent. Stage one is complete," Lord Taoî said, "take your lapdog and head to Mount Fire, and wait for my command."

"As you wish my lord," Michael said as he bowed and left the building. Outside was Christopher Anders and his men on eglîmas. "Let's go!" Michael demanded as he got onto the largest eglîma.

"Where to?" Christopher asked.

"Shut up," Michael slapped Christopher across the face, nearly knocking him off of his eglîma, "lapdog." Michael took off towards Mount Fire. Christopher readjusted himself.

"Well?" he said angrily at his men, who started off after Michael, followed by Christopher.

Lord Taoî was finally alone. Deep in the Hedia Mountains, he planned his next move. Suddenly, he sensed two people approaching the mountains. Before they could even start climbing, the two were suddenly standing in front of a building located in the heart of the mountains.

"Come on you numoni," a female said as she pulled Father Izea into the building.

"Wh, wh, where are you taking me?" Father Izea asked nervously.

"Silence," the woman said as she pulled his chains, nearly causing him to fall. Before he knew it, they were standing in a large rounded room with a dark figure standing along the side.

"And who do we have here?" the figure asked.

"The numoni Father Izea, my lord." the woman bowed. From the darkness, the figure emerged. Lord Taoî was alive, very much alive.

"Very good Mariah Flamington," he said as he approached Father Izea. The moment Lord Taoî approached Father Izea, he immediately fell to his knees. Lord Taoî started laughing.

"Now that's more like it," he chuckled. Father Izea just stared at the ground, shivering with pure fear. "Oh and look.... he's shivering," Lord Taoî chuckled even harder. He stopped chuckling and bent down to Father Izea's face, pulling it up from the ground to his face, "boo." Father Izea squealed and cowered in fear at just the sight of Lord Taoî. Immediately, Lord Taoî started chuckling again. "Oh, you pathetic hiumäns," he said as he stood up, "always cowering behind fear…. I love it!" He stopped chuckling. "Take him away," he ordered.

"As you wish, my lord," Mariah said as she rose. "Come on you numoni," she stated as she yanked him up and pulled him away. Lord Taoî was alone once again.

"Now for stage two," he said. Suddenly, pure Darkness filled the room and just like that, it was gone along with Lord Taoî.

Michael and Christopher barely made it to the top of Mount Fire when pure Darkness appeared. Lord Taoî emerged and the pure Darkness dissipated.

"My lord," Michael said as Christopher, his men, and himself bowed.

"Come," Lord Taoî said as he headed towards the lava. Once at the edge, Lord Taoî started chanting.

"Kurël te du, to que peze lo lu yito amaze de Kurëlzirlo." Suddenly, the lava started to boil. From the depths of the lava rose a creature made entirely of lava.

"What is that?" Christopher asked, a bit nervous.

"A Kurëlzirlo," Lord Taoî said with a smile on his face, from Kurël."

"Rrrrroooaarrrr," the creature busted out, "mmmaaasterrr." Lord Taoî just chuckled.

"Go to the Eastern Mountains and find the entrance to the Labyrinth," he ordered.

"Rrrrroooaarrrr," the creature answered and started off towards the mountains. Smiling, Lord Taoî snapped his fingers and pure Darkness appeared. Lord Taoî stepped into the Darkness and both himself and the pure Darkness disappeared.

Pure Darkness appeared and Lord Taoî stepped out. While he looked at the ocean, the Darkness disappeared.

"Gilë te du, to que peze lo lu yito amaze de Rëptissh," Lord Taoî chanted. The water below started turning, spinning inward. Suddenly, a Rëptissh emerged. "Go! Seek out the entrance!" Lord Taoî ordered. The creature didn't make a sound. It just stood there, staring at him. "Stupid creature," he snarled as he began waving his hand counterclockwise. The spinning water slowly stopped as a cloud of pure Darkness appeared around one of the creature's arms. Suddenly, the cloud transformed into a bracelet looking device and latched itself onto the arm. The creature let out a horrifying screech.

"I said, seek out the entrance!" Lord Taoî ordered again. The creature let out another screech then started heading towards the Vinn Forest. Pure Darkness appeared behind Lord Taoî. "Four down, two to go," he chuckled as he stepped into the Darkness, as he disappeared, so did the pure Darkness.

Lord Taoî started chuckling, "Now this will be easy." Deep in the Rocky Region, he stood high on a mountain top overlooking other mountain tops. With a snap of his finger, one mountain top began to shift and move. It transformed and reformed itself as a Gollunm.

"You know what to do," he said to the creature, which turned around and headed towards Tii.

Back on Mount Fire, Michael and Christopher watched as the Kurëlzirlo head towards the Eastern Mountains.

"Aaaaa!" shouted Michael as he fell to his knees, grasping his chest in pain.

"Sir? What's wrong?" Christopher asked as he tried to help. Mr. Cashner shoved Christopher out of the way and quickly took off his shirt. A small burn mark appeared in the center of this chest.

"What did you do?" Christopher asked.

"Nothing," he said as the pain subsided, "nothing." He started to wonder if Lord Taoî had poisoned him, but it was actually worse than that. He put his shirt back on and got up. Christopher tried to help. "I got it," he said. The two then headed down the mountain to meet up with Mariah.

Back at Moonshiar, the two met up with Mariah in the prison cells.

"Get in there you filthy numoni," she snarled as she shoved Father Izea into a cell.

"Who's that?" Christopher asked.

"Some numoni who gave away the locations to the entrances to the labyrinth," she said as she locked the cell, "a very big help to us."

"Indeed," Michael agreed as Father Izea turned around. The three chuckled, thinking Darkness was going to finally win as they left the room. Father Izea felt so disappointed in himself. He never meant to put anyone in danger. He got up and tried to wiggle the door free, but it was no use.

"Who's there?" came a woman's voice from behind him. He immediately turned around and stared into the shadows in front of him.

"My, my, my name is Father Izea. Who, who are you?" he asked, very nervously. Two figures began to emerge into the light. It was a couple, a man and a woman.

"We are Mr. and Mrs. Steven and Doreen Shaw," the man said. Drake's parents were alive....

Chapter Four:

Stage One

Drake seemed restless as he tried to sleep. The next day was the first stage of the games and he needed all of his strength. After tossing and turning for hours, he finally decided to get up and take a walk. He walked all the way down to the level where the stages were to be held. He walked to the northern part of the first level. A small river came from behind a wall and ended at a small pond. He walked up to it and knelt next to it. Neither the river nor pond was very deep. At the bottom laid thousands of coins of different shapes and colors. Drake reached into the pond and barely touched the coins when suddenly everything went black. He quickly pulled his hand out and stood up, not knowing what to expect. Suddenly, the luminätas relit themselves. Drake heard noises coming from the way into the level. Then, all of a sudden half of the contestants came running into the northern part. They all darted for the coins in the river and pond. They were looking for a certain coin. As soon as each person found one, they automatically won that stage and were allowed to leave. Only eighty out of the one hundred contestants can move on. Then, just like before, the lights went out and it became dead silent. The luminätas relit and Drake found himself kneeling back down next to the pond with his hand still in the water. He looked around but no one was there. He was still alone. Drake wondered what happened. Could that have been his sitilou powers? Did he just have a vision of the future and how to win the first stage? Drake was confused and a little scared. He left the level and returned home, hoping to rest this time.

All the contestants arrived in the arena as the fans cheered them on.

"Welcome! Welcome!" Oshwaia said as the fans began to calm. He waited until the crowd was completely quiet. "Welcome to Stage One contestants. To begin with, each of you has received a number. Remember that number. Now, Father Brai will explain the rules." Oshwaia took a few steps back and Father Brai came up.

"To start off, each stage will test a specific skill, but will push you one way or another." He paused and took a breath. "Now, for Stage One. When you reach the first level, odd numbers will go south and even numbers will go north. Each of you will need to find a coin with your number printed in blue on it. Once the first eighty contestants bring their coins back here to the arena, they move onto Stage

Two. Prepare for the signal and good luck." Drake looked at his number; 32. Jessica got 87 and Lance got 91. Drake took the card with his number on it and put it in his pocket. He turned around to prepare himself. Others joined him and just like that, all of the contestants were facing the entrance of the arena, waiting for the gates to open. The moment the gates began to open, one of the contestants took off towards it, followed by everyone else and Stage One began.

Once on the first level, Drake ran as fast as he could to the North part. There were already some contestants inside looking for the coins. Drake automatically went straight for the pond. Like in his vision, there were the coins, scattered throughout the bottom of the river and pond. He knelt down and started searching for his coin.

"Hey, he found them!" a contestant shouted as she pointed at Drake. *Crap!* Drake thought to himself. Everyone in the room suddenly came running towards the river and pond. It became almost instantly impossible for Drake to find his coin. Suddenly, out of Drake's right eye, he caught a glimpse of a coin shining brighter than the rest. After taking a deep breath, he took a chance and went for the coin. As soon as he touched it, something happened.

The moment Drake touched the coin, everything around him suddenly froze. This scared Drake to a point where he dropped the coin. Things suddenly began moving again. This intrigued him. He touched the coin again and the same thing happened; everything stopped, as if time itself and everything in it froze. After picking up the coin, Drake carefully made his way back towards the arena. As he entered the arena, Oshwaia was there to congratulate him.

"Oshwaia, what are you doing here? Why aren't you frozen like the rest?" Drake asked surprised.

"I am the one who created this spell, because there is something extremely urgent to show you," Oshwaia answered.

"What spell?" Drake was getting more and more confused.

"The spell to freeze time, but we must hurry. Time is of the essence," Oshwaia said as he hurried out of the arena and towards the temple. Drake followed close behind.

Once at the very top, the two entered the room.

"Please?" Oshwaia said, pointing at the stone table. Drake placed his hand on the table but this time, his Tërcerlin symbol started glowing white. The Tërcerlin symbol on the table started glowing white and a white cloud appeared above the table.

"We have a numoni in our mists," Oshwaia started, "Father Izea has given in to the powers of Darkness." Suddenly, a vision started to appear in the cloud. "Due to Father Izea's actions, the barriers will soon fail and Lord Taoî and Darkness will come," Oshwaia spoke as Drake watched different creatures and beasts like the Rëptissh and the Syclore heading right for the labyrinth's entrances, commanded by Lord Taoî himself.

"Can....can we stop this?" Drake asked, shocked and scared.

"No," Oshwaia said in a serious tone. Drake was now truly afraid.

"What....what....," Drake started to ask, "what do we do?

"You have been mastering all of the 'Ancient Ways'," Oshwaia replied, "you must master all of them in order to truly defeat Lord Taoî."

"I understand," Drake assured him.

"Good. Now quickly; you must hurry back to where you found the coin!" Oshwaia warned.

"But," Drake started to say.

"Go!" demanded Oshwaia. Without further hesitation, Drake left as quickly as he could.

As soon as he got back to exactly where he found the coin, Drake heard Oshwaia's voice speaking inside his head.

"Drop the coin into the water then pick it back up," it said. Drake did so. He held the coin out over the water then he let go. The moment the coin hit the bottom of the river, time unfroze and the contestants went back to picking up the coins.

Drake bent down and picked up his coin but this time, nothing happened. Time kept going.

"Look, he found his coin already," one contestant said.

"Ah man, no fair!" said another. Instantly, Drake knew what to do. He ran as fast as he could to the arena, where the crowd waited for the first contestant to arrive. The crowd began to cheer and roar as Drake entered the arena. Drake looked up at the judges, where Oshwaia was, nodding in congrats. Shortly after, three more contestants entered the arena, where the crowd continued to cheer and roar. Soon eighty contestants including Drake, Jessica, and Lance were all in the arena. Oshwaia stood up and stepped forward. He waved his hand for silence, which the crowd obeyed.

"First, let us give a big round of applause for the eighty contestants who will be moving onto Stage Two." The crowd began cheering and roaring. After a moment, he calmed them down. "And let's give it up for the twenty who will not be continuing on," Oshwaia continued. The crowd cheered and roared again. "Stage Two will commence in two days. Thank you all." He took a step back and the crowd cheered and roared yet again.

Chapter Five:

A Hidden Truth

Drake laid in his bed, staring at the ceiling.

"Drake, are you awake?" Zack asked. Thanks to a spell created by Oshwaia, Father Brai, Father Paul, and Drake himself, now had the ability to speak to Zack using their thoughts.

"What do you mean?" he asked without moving. Zack, in his silver wolf form came up to Drake.

"You haven't been yourself since Stage One," he answered. Instantly, Drake thought back to during the time of Stage One, where Oshwaia and himself were in the temple. Second per second replayed inside his head about what was happening above them all. He decided it was time to tell his best friend.

"Father Izea has betrayed all of us," Drake said as he continued to blankly stare at the ceiling.

"What do you mean?"

"Father Izea has given into Darkness and went to the surface." Dead silence filled the room. "By going to the surface, he broke one of the barriers, causing the rest to weaken. Lord Taoî has sent different creatures and beasts to the entrances to get us." Zack didn't know what to say. He was shocked and stunned.

"How….how much time do we have?" Zack finally asked.

"I don't know," Drake replied.

"Shouldn't we tell the others?"

"Yes but if we do, the news could spread and mass chaos would occur."

"You're right, but what do we do?"

"I don't know yet." Silence filled the room again. Suddenly, a knock came from Drake's door.

"Drake?" came Jessica's voice from the other side of the door, "are you still awake?" Drake quickly got up.

"Not a word," he whispered to Zack, who nodded in agreement. Drake hurried to the door and opened it.

"Hey Jess, yeah I'm still awake," he told her, "what's up?"

"I had a really bad nightmare and for some reason, I needed to see you," she told him.

"Oh," Drake replied, a bit surprised. "Yeah. Come in, come in," he told her as he moved aside for her to enter.

"Thank you," she said as she walked in. She looked around a moment. Although it was a bit small, it felt rather homey and peaceful. Zack got up from next to Drake's bed and wandered over to his own bed Drake made for him. He laid down and fell right to sleep. Drake made his bed and offered Jessica a spot on it. The two sat down together.

"Thank you again," she said.

"No problem," he replied, "so what was the nightmare about?"

"Well," she began, "it all started at the end ceremony. The ground began to rumble, people started panicking, and everywhere you looked was chaos. All of us found each other except for you."

47

"Me?" Drake asked surprisingly.

"You were nowhere to be found; like you had just suddenly disappeared. Then, it all stopped; the rumbling, the panicking, and the chaos. Moments of pure silence past before he came barging in."

"Lord Taoî," Drake interrupted. Jessica just continued.

"But it wasn't just him. He brought all kinds of creatures and beasts with him, to enslave us all. But the worst part was the Darkness that followed." Drake knew exactly what this meant, but was what Jessica saw really the future? "May I stay with you tonight?" Jessica asked. Without hesitation, Drake said yes and the two got in Drake's bed. Jessica wrapped herself around Drake for warmth, as Drake held her close. Little did Drake know, something about the two of them together felt right to Jessica.

"Good night Drake," she said as she slowly faded off to sleep.

"Good night Jessica," he replied back then gave her a gentle kiss on the head. He stared at the ceiling again but this time, with more questions than ever before.

The next day, Jessica and Zack were woken up by the delicious smells of a home cooked meal. The two got up and wandered over to the table. It was set and completely covered with food, but only enough for two. The two looked around but Drake was nowhere to be seen. Where was he?

Meanwhile, down in a secret hidden chamber, Oshwaia was training Drake on the 'Ancient Ways'.

"Again," Oshwaia said sternly. Drake closed his eyes and tried to concentrate. The ground rumbled a little and a small rock shot out of the ground and hovered as Drake's Tërcerlin symbol glowed green. A fireball suddenly appeared in Drake's hand. He opened his eyes and aimed at the hovering rock. He shot the fireball at the rock, but nearly missing the rock; hitting it on the top-left side. Angered with frustration, he let the rock drop, crumbling instantly it hit the ground.

"What is bothering you?" Oshwaia asked as he invited Drake to sit next to him. Drake, somewhat out of breath, accepted Oshwaia's invite. He sat next to Oshwaia and took a deep breath.

"Jessica came to my place last night," Drake started off, "she was saying she had a nightmare and when she told me of it….," Drake paused.

"What is it my child?" Oshwaia asked. Drake was too scared to tell him but knew he had to.

"She said Lord Taoî somehow breaks through the barriers and is coming to enslave us all." Oshwaia was so shocked he had to stand up. "What's wrong?" Drake asked as he shot up to catch Oshwaia.

"This is bad," was all Oshwaia could say. Silence quickly filled the training room. Both Oshwaia and Drake knew exactly what needed to happen so Drake went back to practicing.

Chapter Six:

Stage Two

On the morning of Stage Two, Drake did not want to get up.

"Drake, wake up," Zack said as he licked Drake's face, "or you'll be late for Stage Two." He stopped licking to allow his words to sink into Drake's thoughts.

"Stage Two," Drake thought to himself, "....Stage Two....." Silence quickly filled the room. "Stage Two!" Drake shouted as he sprung forward. Zack freaked out because Drake had scared him. After calming him down, the two got ready. *Knock Knock* Someone knocked on Drake's door. He hurried over to the door and opened it.

"Good morning Drake," said Father Brai.

"Good morning Father," Drake replied, "come in."

"Thank you," he said as he entered the room. "I'd like to talk to you on the way to the arena, if you wouldn't mind."

"Not at all," Drake replied as he shut the door, "let me finish getting ready and then we can leave." Father Brai nodded his head in agreeance and Drake finished getting ready to go.

On the way to the arena, Father Brai spoke quickly yet quietly.

"I don't have much time to tell you this Drake," he began.

"Tell me what?" Drake interrupted.

"I'm not supposed to help the contestants in any way," he continued, "that's why I'm helping a friend instead." He stopped and smiled at Drake, who smiled back. Father Brai bent down to Drake's level. "Remember this, don't touch the white."

Instantly, Drake got confused. What did he mean by don't touch the white? He stood back up.

"Father Brai," shouted Father Paul as he spotted the three heading towards the arena, "good morning." Instantly, he started walking over.

"Good morning Father Paul," Father Brai said as Father Paul approached them.

"Good morning," Drake and Zack said as well.

"Are you ready for today Drake?" Father Paul asked him.

"I hope so," Drake replied. Then, everyone laughed. After separating, Drake headed to the arena where the other contestants were gathering.

"Welcome! Welcome!" Oshwaia began. The cheering crowd started dying down. "Welcome to Stage Two contestants. To begin with, Father Paul will explain this stage's rules." Oshwaia backed up and Father Paul stood up and took the podium.

"Contestants, hidden with the sands are four kinds of stones; red, blue, yellow, and green. Each stone will represent a ground in the next stage. The first sixty contestants to bring back a stone will move onto Stage Three. Prepare for the signal and best of luck to you all," proclaimed Father Paul. He took his seat and Oshwaia approached again. He waited a moment. Drake looked up towards Oshwaia and the others. He started to look away when he noticed Father Brai starring right at him. Father Brai nodded at Drake, hoping he'd know what he was referring to. Just then, Oshwaia nodded and the gates opened. Contestants started running towards the gates and Stage Two began.

Drake suddenly stopped as he walked into the southern part of the level. Sand filled both rooms and piles of white sand seemed to be scattered across the parts.

"Don't touch the white," Father Brai's voice rang inside Drake's head. Contestants all around him were searching for the stones.

"I found one!" a contestant shouted as he found one while digging through a pile of white sand. Suddenly, everyone in that part went searching within the white piles. Drake tried to stop several contestants but no one listened. Then, one by one, each contestant fell; unconscious. As several contestants fell, they dropped their stones. Drake ran up to a red stone and picked it up. All of a sudden, something moved within the white sand in front of him. Drake froze in his steps. He waited a moment but nothing moved. He slowly turned around started heading out when something moved behind him, again. Drake immediately turned back around.

"Who….who's there?" Drake shouted. Something moved in front of him. It started from within the pile of white sand and darted right for Drake. It hit the yellow sand, circled around him, and then suddenly disappeared in front of him. Drake took a few steps back. A creature busted out from behind him, causing him to fall forward. Immediately, he turned around and backed up as far as he could. The look on Drake's face was pure terror. This creature, with its pure black eyes, snakelike head, and centipede-like body, was out to kill and Drake was next.

He ran as fast as he could but the creature tripped him. Drake turned around and tried to crawl backwards but the dypiroos grabbed him instead. Instantly, he blasted a fireball at the creature's body, injuring it and causing it to let go of him. He fell, quickly got up, and tried to escape.

He ran and ran, around the way up and down the stages and into the other part of the level.

"Drake?" Jessica shouted as he entered the room.

"Jessica?" Drake shouted as he ran towards her, across the sand. They hugged as the two met.

"What's going on Drake? Why are we the only ones not frozen?" Jessica asked.

"I don't know but there's a," Drake started to say when suddenly, the dypiroos darted into the room, still after Drake and now after Jessica too.

"What is that?" she screamed as the two of them ran and the creature followed.

"I don't know but we need to kill it. It's dark, I can feel it," Drake answered. He suddenly stopped, turned around, and shot another fireball at it. The creature screeched in pain. He shot two more fireballs, trying to injure the creature. The creature let out a horrifying screech, causing Drake and Jessica to cover their ears.

"How do we stop this thing?" Jessica asked. Drake shot a few more fireballs at it, causing two arms to fall off. As soon as they hit the ground, they disintegrated into a tiny cloud of smoke then just dissipated. The two looked at each other with relief because they knew how to defeat this creature. As the dypiroos screeched in pain, it lunged at its prey.

"Enough!" Drake shouted as it came towards them. This creature angered Drake so much that instead of firing another fireball at it, Drake created an ice-ball, turning the creature into pure ice from head to the very last hand. To finish things for good, Drake then shot a large fireball at the creature, causing it to crumble and fall. Just like the hands, the entire creature disintegrated into a large cloud of smoke then dissipated. Drake and

Jessica hugged in relief. Then, all of a sudden, time started again as though it never even froze.

"Give it up for our sixty contestants who will be moving onto Stage Three," Oshwaia announced. The crowd cheered with excitement. "I want to thank the contestants who did not move on, good job." The crowd cheered even more. After calming down, Oshwaia continued, "that concludes Stage Two. Stage Three will be in two days' time so go, rest, and best of luck." The crowd cheered and roared. After the closing of Stage Two, Drake and Jessica immediately sought out Oshwaia, Father Brai, Father Paul, and Father Mika. They explained what exactly happened.

"That's it then," Father Brai concluded.

"What is?" Father Mika asked.

"We are no longer safe down here," Oshwaia warned.

"And I think Father Izea has betrayed us all," Prince Evergreen butted in as he randomly showed up.

"What do you mean?" Jessica asked.

"Well, I've been looking for Father Izea for a few days now and I can't find him anywhere." Oshwaia and Drake looked at each other for they knew exactly where he was. Oshwaia then nodded at Drake.

"We think Father Izea has given into Darkness and broke one of the labyrinth's entrances," Drake finally said. Luckily, no one else was around. "And because of him, it has weakened the others," Drake finished. There was a brief pause.

"We need to tell everyone," Jessica finally said to break the silence, "if Darkness is really coming, we all need to be ready." Sadly, the rest agreed with her but how to let everyone know without causing panic and mayhem was the real task.

Chapter Seven:

The Threat Of Darkness

Tomorrow morning, please meet in
the Tessr Games Arena. This
announcement is for EVERYONE so
please be there.

Father Brai

Things were looking serious when Drake received his flyer. It was only the day after Stage Two and Oshwaia and the others were trying hard to keep things safe.

"Hey Drake?" Kim asked.

"Yeah?" he responded.

"Do you know what this flyer is about?"

"I have no idea," he lied. He hated lying to anyone but she would find out soon.

"Come on Drake or we'll be late again," Jessica said.

"Late, late for what?" Kim asked.

"Training for the games," Drake answered, "I'll talk to you later." Drake and Jessica then left Kim's home and headed off to training.

"Look, I said I was sorry," Father Izea said as he continued to beg for mercy.

"There is no forgiveness for what you have done Father Izea," Doreen stated firmly as she sat as far away from him as possible.

"But," Father Izea started to say.

"But what?" Doreen interrupted, "you have put every living being's life on the line for your own personal gain; your prince, our son."

"We are so ashamed to have even met such a man," Steven chimed in, holding his wife. Father Izea bowed his head in shame, for breaking a seal really did give Lord Taoî the break he needed.

"Good, good," Oshwaia said as Jessica had Drake pinned to the ground.

"Lucky shot," Drake said as Jessica got off of him.

"Luck had nothing to do with it," she jokingly said as she helped him up.

"You two have come such a long ways," Father Brai said as he and a guest entered the training room.

"Father Brai," Drake and Jessica shouted simultaneously with excitement.

"What are you doing here?" Drake asked.

"Drake, Jessica, I would like to introduce you to Father Sage," Father Brai said as he introduced his guest.

"It's a pleasure to meet you both," Father Sage said, "I've heard much about you two, all good mind you."

"Well that's good," Drake said as everyone started laughing. After a bit of laughter, things got serious.

"Father Sage is here to replace Father Izea. His ceremony will be this evening before tomorrow's announcement," Father Brai stated.

"I thought Father Mika was replacing Father Izea," Drake asked.

"Only for Stage Two he was," Father Brai stated.

"Oh okay," replied Drake. Silence suddenly filled the room.

"Well, we must finish preparing for tomorrow," Father Sage said to break the silence.

"Yes, right. Well, off we go then," Father Brai responded.

"I shall join you," Oshwaia started off, "great job today you two. We shall resume tomorrow after the announcement."

"Okay, thank you," Drake said. Father Brai, Father Sage, Oshwaia, and Jessica started to leave when Jessica noticed Drake wasn't leaving.

"Are you coming Drake?" she asked as she rejoined him.

"Yeah, you go on ahead," Drake said with a smile on his face.

"Oh okay," Jessica responded and turned to leave.

"Hey! After everyone is asleep, meet me at the highest point of the temple," Drake whispered as he stopped her, still smiling. She turned to him, nodded, and smiled, then left the room. This was Drake's chance to finally tell her how he truly feels about her and he didn't want to mess things up.

After she knew everyone was asleep, Jessica snuck out of bed and headed towards the temple. Climbing up the temple in the middle of the night seemed creepy yet peaceful to her. She climbed to the highest point, searching for Drake.

"Drake?" Jessica whispered as she searched. At the very top of the temple was a small lookout type platform. You could practically see the entire labyrinth from that height and at one of the corners looking out into the labyrinth was Drake.

"Drake?" she whispered again, just to make sure it was him. He turned towards her and smiled.

"Hey," he said softly. The lights around the two seemed to glisten in his eyes. "Come here," he said as he waved her over. She walked over to him and the two sat down, admiring the view. The luminätas produced enough light to barely reach the top of the labyrinth's walls but the pockets of light above the temple produced just a little more light.

"You know," Drake started the conversation off, "five years ago, I would have never imagined me being 'The Chosen One' or Lord Taoî being released and Darkness taking over or even getting the chance to meet someone like you."

"Like me?" Jessica asked.

"You're smart and funny," he paused and chuckled a little, "you're also witty and cunning as well as beautiful." Instantly, Jessica started blushing.

"Oh Drake," she said, starting to become embarrassed.

"I'm serious Jessica," he paused, "you are very beautiful. You make me feel happy and wanted and…. and I think I like you."

"Like me?"

"Yeah." Silence fell over the two.

"Well I think I like you too," Jessica said with the biggest smile ever.

"Really?" Drake asked, kind of shocked.

"Really," she said as the two got really close to each other. They looked at each other with a spark of passion in their eyes. They leaned in to kiss one another for the first time when Drake caught a glimpse of something in the distance as he was closing his eyes to kiss her. He quickly pulled back and got up. Jessica opened her eyes and had a confused looked on her face.

"What's wrong Drake?" she asked.

"There's," he paused as he walked to a different corner and stared out into the distance. Jessica quickly got up and joined him.

"There's what?" she asked, very confused.

"There's something out there," he said as he pointed towards the Labyrinth Arena. There was something in that direction but it wasn't good; it served the Darkness.

As Drake and Jessica got to the base of the temple, they ran into Oshwaia.

"Oshwaia, something is in," Drake started to say.

"The Labyrinth Arena and it's a hyîdrai," Oshwaia unintentionally interrupted him.

"What's a hyîdrai?" Drake asked

"Didn't either one of you know Father Izea?"

"No."

"Not really," Jessica answered, "he kept to himself mostly. Why?"

"I hardly knew him myself," Oshwaia started, "but I did know he was working on creating new creatures for food and labor."

"Creatures?" Jessica asked.

"I'll explain on the way but we must hurry," Oshwaia said as he started to head to the living/housing level. The other two were right behind. "Father Izea was working on several creatures; the bikra were to produce meat, the yinre were to produce feces to help fertilize the ground better, and the jemorra were to help us fight the dark creatures Lord Taoî and Darkness has waiting for us. They were all magnificent creatures with the purest of souls....," Oshwaia stopped speaking.

"What happened? Did he succeed?" Jessica asked.

"That he did my dear, or well, to a degree. See, Father Izea was missing some type of ingredient because the creatures turned out only three feet high. He was very angry and frustrated. He had each creature locked up tight, each in its own room." By this point of the story, the three had made it to the living/housing level and were heading towards Sector C. They walked right past Father Izea's place and instantly, Drake became very confused.

"Where are we going?" he asked. Jessica wanted to know too.

"You'll see, but we must keep hurrying," Oshwaia insisted. The three entered Sector C-1 and headed right to Prince Evergreen's home. *Knock Knock, Knock Knock* Oshwaia knocked.

"What if he's not awake?" Drake asked only to be answered by the door opening by Prince Evergreen.

"We have a dire situation that may require your assistance," Oshwaia disclosed softly, trying not to wake others around them.

"How can I help?" he asked.

"It has to do with Father Izea's creatures," Oshwaia stated. Prince Evergreen immediately shut his door and the four raced quietly to Father Izea's home. Once inside, Prince Evergreen pulled a book from a bookshelf and a secret passage way appeared, which led to Father Izea's creature room. In the room, there were a few openings in the wall with bar doors and a table in the center of the room. On the table were several journal books of Father Izea's work. Drake skimmed through one until he stopped on a certain entry:

Log 665:

My experiment has gone horribly wrong. I tried very hard to combine the bikra, yinre, and the jemorra to create the perfect creature, but instead of a perfect creature, I created one with a soul as pure as Darkness itself; a hyîdrai…. Immediately, I destroyed it and buried the remains in the

Labyrinth Arena. Pray to the great Queen
Evë its soul finds peace.

"Hey, look at this," Drake said as he showed the others.

"That creature must be the hyîdrai," Jessica said as she finished reading the entry.

"We must hurry and destroy it for good," Prince Evergreen stated.

"Before anyone else finds out and creates terror and chaos," Drake said. Everyone definitely agreed with him. Taking Father Izea's journals about these creatures with them, the four of them left his home and hurried as quickly as possible to the Labyrinth Arena.

The hyîdrai had destroyed pretty much most of the Labyrinth Arena and had started on the labyrinth's walls.

"We need to destroy this thing NOW!" Prince Evergreen said in fear.

"We will," Drake said calmly, "but first, we must find its weak points."

"Good thinking," Oshwaia said.

"But how do we do that?" Prince Evergreen asked, still very frightened. Drake opened one of Father Izea's journals and started looking through it until he came across log number 483.

He started reading the log out loud, "Log 483; I noticed some odd behaviors in the bikra. It seems to dislike the cold, or anything cold for that fact. Its legs tend to tense up and it is hard for it to move."

"Cold, good to know," Jessica said. Drake continued through the journal until he found another log.

"Log 493," he started reading, "the yinre reacts oddly to red berries. It upsets the stomach, which in turns weakens its fighting skills. The only way to activate the berry's effect is to punch it in the stomach after it has consumed some. The effect nearly paralyzes the creature only for a few minutes, then it returns to normal."

"Cold and paralyzing berries," Prince Evergreen started off, "good combination."

"I agree," Oshwaia said. Drake looked though a different journal to find more weaknesses.

"Log 580; I have come to notice that the bikra and the yinre cannot be within the same area for a long period of time. The smell of the yinre's feces is too much for the bikra that it causes it to get angry and starts attacking the yinre."

"That's disgusting!" Prince Evergreen said, trying not to gag at the thought of feces.

"But useful," Drake said then continued through the journal for the creature's weakness. "Found it!" he said as he stopped on log 626.

"Log 626; the jemorra is turning out to be a magnificent creature, stunning and intelligent as can be, except for one small yet dangerous flaw. The jemorra behaves strangely around the color dark blue. I'm not sure why but the color dark blue makes the creature become distracted, and I mean distracted."

"What does he mean distracted?" Jessica asked.

"I'm not sure," Oshwaia answered, "but we need to figure out how to stop the creature and fast."

"Drake?" Jessica asked, "any ideas?" This was exactly what he had been training for. A smile grew on Drake's face.

"I have a few," he said and closed the journal.

Chapter Eight:

Defeating The Hyîdrai

"Aaaaah!" Prince Evergreen shouted as they were nearly crushed upon entering the Labyrinth Arena.

"Whatever you have planned, you better do it quickly," Jessica said as they quickly got up.

"Hey! Hey!" Drake shouted as he ran towards the hyîdrai.

"Be careful," Jessica whispered to herself as Drake ran into action.

"Hey!" Drake continued to shout. Before he knew it, the creature was heading right for him. "Oooh crap!" he said as he took off running even faster. Drake honestly had no idea what to do, but he had to come up with something and quick.

"Cold, good to know," Jessica's words rang in his head. "Cold," it rang again.

"Cold!" Drake shouted with excitement as he turned around. The hyîdrai was right behind him. "Freeze!" he shouted as ice came from Drake's palms as he pointed them right at the creature. Instantly, it started freezing. As the ice branched out, Drake pulled out his Irrösa sword. The hyîdrai had become a solid block of ice. "Now to destroy this thing once and for all," Drake said as he started swinging at the creature. As each body part fell, it shattered into pieces. By the time Drake was done, the hyîdrai was no more than a pile of slowly melting cut up body parts.

"You did it Drake!" Prince Evergreen shouted delightfully.

"I never doubted you, my child," Oshwaia congratulated him.

"Same here!" Jessica agreed.

"It's over, it's finally over," Prince Evergreen said with a sigh of relief.

"I'm sorry Prince Evergreen," Drake said, "but this is far from over."

"What, what do you mean Drake?" Prince Evergreen asked, somewhat confused and yet, somewhat concerned.

"Oshwaia," Drake said as he turned towards him, "you said that the barriers will no longer hold, is that right?"

"Yes," Oshwaia replied.

"Then Jessica," Drake said as he turned towards her, "what you saw about Lord Taoî must be true and we are all in grave danger."

Every single hiumän was in the Tessr Games Arena when the news finally came.

"Ladies and gentlemen," Oshwaia said as he started to quiet the crowd. "Ladies and gentlemen," he said again a little louder. The crowd quieted down to a dead silence. "I would like to introduce to you all Drake Shaw," he introduced Drake. The crowd clapped as he took the stage.

"Ladies and gentlemen, we have called you all here today to inform you of a great problem we all face. Father Izea, a beloved friend and family member....," he paused a moment, "he.... he has betrayed us all." Instantly, a little bit of anger and fear broke out in the crowd.

"Silence!" shouted Oshwaia and instantly, the crowd obeyed.

"He has broken one of the six seals that protect us down here and has surrendered himself over to Darkness and Lord Taoî himself," Drake continued. Dead silence flooded the arena. "Soon, the other barriers will break and Lord Taoî," he took a breath because he didn't want to say it but knew he had to, "Lord Taoî will come." Panic and chaos started to break out all over. Drake honestly didn't know what to do until the right words came inside his head.

"Listen please!" Drake shouted, trying to calm the crowd down but it was only making things worse. Drake instantly made a ball of rock appear from the arena's floor and shot it upwards, catching most of everyone's attention but to truly get everyone's attention, he created a fireball and shot it at the flying rock. The rock shattered into thousands of pieces and went straight downward. This definitely caught everyone's attention. "Look, I know from firsthand experience how scary and confusing this may be, but look at us. Yeah, Lord Taoî was released five years ago, but we have been striving, living, these past five years. That right there says a lot about our species." Mumbles of good words started to spread throughout the crowd. "And, if he was trapped once, who's not to say he can't be trapped again?"

"Yeah," sounds of agreeance started to come from the crowd.

"What do you say? Let us unite! Let us become one strong species. Let US, take down Lord Taoî, once and for all!" Drake shouted with full determination.

"Yeah, let's do it!" shouted people from the crowd. Within moments, the entire crowd was cheering and shouting, all on Drake's side. Drake looked over at his friends, who were smiling and cheering him on. Drake didn't smile back, for he knew that the real games had only just begun.

Chapter Nine:

Stage Three

"Welcome! Welcome!" Oshwaia shouted as he tried to calm the roaring crowd. The crowd almost suddenly calmed down and began to listen. "Contestants, welcome to Stage Three. Today, Father Mika will explain this stage's rules," he said then backed up and Father Mika stood up and took the podium.

"Today's stage will be challenging but also fun," Father Mika began. "To start off, pull out the stones from the previous stage. Contestants with red and yellow stones group to the right and contestants with blue and green stones group to the left." The contestants grouped as he ordered. "Now, group into individual groups based on the color of your stones but still on the same side you are currently on." Again, the contestants obeyed. "Most of you are aware of the fun childhood game called capture the flag. Well today, that is exactly what you will be playing, only with fun and exciting challenges. The first challenge is the groups standing next to you are your rivals; blue verses green which will go first, followed by red verses yellow." Jessica was in the green group while Drake was in the yellow group. While looking around, Drake noticed Lance was in the red group; his rival team. "In the second challenge, you will not only be playing capture the flag, but you will also be facing the next elimination. Each of you will be equipped with a lupimas gun filled with your group's color lupimas. The group with the most amount of members hit out of all four teams will not move onto Stage Four. Have fun and best of luck." Father Mika ended and took his seat. Helpers of the games passed out specific colored lupimas guns to each group. Soon, each contestant was ready for Stage Three. Oshwaia retook the podium.

"With every contestant ready, will the blue and green groups head down to prepare while the red and yellow groups wait here for your turn. Wait for the signal and best of luck."

"Good luck Jessica," Drake said as he hugged her as she walked by.

"Thanks," she said as she hugged him back. Then she headed off with her group to hide their flag and prepare to begin.

Jessica took several deep breaths before darting for the blue team's area. She slowly snuck around the stairs when about halfway around, several of her team members came running up to join her.

"Hey, may we join you?" a team member asked her.

"Sure," she replied. To her, the more the merrier because the more of her team members on the other side, the more of a distraction they will cause. The group then darted for the blue side. Three team members got hit as they entered, causing the group to split up; exactly what Jessica wanted. Her and three other team members ran as fast as they could over the sand and hid behind a pillar. Jessica looked around and realized it was the same level as Stage Two, only they added pillars to hide behind and raised the piles of white sand. One team member went running up the hill they were hiding next to as Jessica and the rest went behind the hill. They all met up behind another pillar. Luckily, no one was hit, yet. They saw another pillar and darted for it. *Bang* one team member was hit; *Bang Bang* two more struck down. Jessica's plan was working perfectly. Hiding behind the pillar, the group was looking and suggesting ways to go when Jessica barely saw the blue team's flag waving behind a pillar in the distance. The group decided to split into two smaller groups; one to the pillar on the left of them and the other to the pillar in front of them. Jessica knew going for the front pillar was too risky so she went with the left group. *Bang* one team member heading towards the front pillar was hit; *Bang Bang* followed by two more, leaving only one team member to make it to the front pillar. *Bang* the team member in front of Jessica was hit just as they made it to the pillar.

"You can do it!" the team member told Jessica as he fell to his knees, then all the way. Jessica quickly peaked around the pillar and spotted the blue team's flag directly in front of her, but guarded by three blue team members. She took a deep breath and took off running towards the flag; gun in hands, ready to fire. *Bang Bang* two of the three blue team members were hit, but not by Jessica. She immediately looked over to her right to see one of her team members un-hit, helping her from behind the front pillar. *Bang* the last blue team member guarding the flag was hit. *Bang* but so was the team member that was helping her just as Jessica got to the flag. She immediately grabbed the flag and everything just stopped for at that moment, Jessica and her team won that round, or at least everyone hoped.

"Congratulations to the green team for winning the first round of capture the flag," Oshwaia announced. The crowd cheered and roared. "And let's give it up for the blue team for their efforts," Oshwaia continued, and just like before, the crowd cheered and roared. After calming down, Oshwaia finished, "Now, the red and yellow groups head down and prepare while the blue and green groups stay here and clean up. Wait for the signal and best of luck." Drake was looking right at Oshwaia when he very slightly nodded at Drake, wishing him luck.

       Drake had a small group of nine total team members with him when they left for the yellow side. *Bang* one yellow team member was hit as they entered the way between the two teams. After deciding to go right, they barely passed half way when *Bang* one of Drake's team members was shot. After waiting a moment, they headed out. *Bang Bang* two more of Drake's team members got hit. Just as the two shots were fired, Drake immediately shot a fire in the same direction of the first two. That red team member was hit right in the chest. Drake's team, more alert and vigilant, went forward into the red team's area. *Bang* Drake shot at a red team member who was standing guard. Continuing forward, the team stopped at the first pillar.

"Look!" a member of Drake's team said as she pointed towards the direction of the red team's flag.

"We should split up," another member said.

"I agree," Drake replied. It was settled that two team members would flank north as a distraction while the other four would go right. Just as the two heading north barely got to the pillar, *Bang* one was hit. *Bang Bang* the other red team member fired back. The two shots hit their targets but unfortunately, one of the firing yellow team members shot a fire back simultaneously hitting the red team member. *Bang Bang* two more shots fired by yellow team members, hitting one red team member on the right arm and hitting the other red team member on the right leg, both falling to the ground right in front of Drake. Him and the other yellow team members ran as fast as they could to the next pillar. After all four were behind, they checked each other to see if anyone was hit. Thankfully, no one was hit. They caught their breaths and darted for the next pillar when *Bang* another yellow team member was shot. The remaining three of Drake's team had only one more pillar before the red team's flag. They ran as fast as they could, dodging every fire shot at them. The three safely made it behind the pillar when Drake peaked around it to scope out the area. Dead ahead was the red team's flag and of course, Lance was the one guarding it.

"I'm going in. Cover me," whispered Drake and his yellow team members nodded in agreeance. Instantly, the two started shooting towards the flag and Drake took off towards it.

"Drake!" Lance shouted as Drake surprised him but it was too late. Drake was too close for Lance to protect himself. *Bang* just like that, Lance was hit by Drake himself. Lance fell to his knees as Drake ran up to him.

"Sorry buddy," he said, "better luck next time." Something snapped inside Lance's head that began to grow as hatred and disgust. Then, Drake grabbed the flag and Stage Three was complete.

"Congratulations to the yellow team for winning the second round of capture the flag," Oshwaia announced. The crowd cheered and roared. "And let's give it up for the red team for their efforts," Oshwaia continued, and just like before, the crowd cheered and roared. After the crowd simmered down, Oshwaia continued his speech. "The numbers are in and here they are in order of number of team members hit by their opposing teams. Green team won with seven hits," Oshwaia paused. "Yellow team came in second with eight hits." Oshwaia paused again, "red team came in third with nine hits." He paused one last time, "and blue team came in last with ten hits. Let's give it up for the contestants." The crowd cheered and roared. "Thank you blue team but unfortunately, you will not be continuing on," Oshwaia said as the crowd calmed, "let's hear it for the blue team." The crowd cheered and roared louder. After the crowd calmed, Oshwaia finished, "for the other three teams, you will all be continuing onto Stage Four. This concludes Stage Three. Stage Four is in one days' time so go, rest, and best of luck." Even though the stage was ending, Lance's feelings were started to change and that was only the beginning.

Chapter Ten:

The Calzaniti Statue

Later that night after Stage Three was over, Drake was practicing in the Training Room. Training hard, he was covered in sweat and breathing heavily. As Jessica slowly entered the room, she looked around but only saw Drake.

"Hey Drake," she said, trying not to scare him. Drake quickly turned around.

"Oh, hey Jessica," he said as he stopped training, "what's up?"

"Oh not much, just came to check up on you. What's up with you?"

"Oh not much, just training a little."

"Oh, very nice," Jessica paused, "great job today."

"You too," he replied as he walked over to a towel and started drying off. "I wonder what Stage Four will be like," he said.

"Only the 'fathers' know," Jessica said jokingly. The two laughed at the joke.

"Drake! Jessica!" Kim shouted as she came running in, interrupting their laughter.

"Kim, what's up?" Drake asked.

"Come quickly!" she shouted excitingly, then ran as fast as she could out of the Training Room. Confused, Drake and Jessica ran after her.

Once they were in the temple, the two found Kim standing in front of an enchanted glass case.

"Kim? What's going on?" Drake asked as him and Jessica stopped to catch their breaths.

"Look!" Kim said excitingly as she pointed at the item inside the glass case. Drake and Jessica looked at the object. Inside was this year's winning prize. "It's the."

"Calzaniti Statue," the three of them said simultaneously. They all looked at each other with confusion.

"How do you two know about the statue?" Kim asked, "it was just placed here today."

"I....I don't know," Drake said, trying to figure out how he knew. Jessica on the other hand, instantly had her first day vision.

First, everything went black. Then, just as it went black, it became light again only this time, she wasn't standing next to Drake and Kim in the temple. She was in the crowd at the closing ceremony. The crowd was cheering and roaring as Drake was walking up to receive the Calzaniti Statue.

"Hey, what's going on?" Jessica asked the person to her right but he was completely unresponsive. "Hello?" she said as she tried to touch him to get his attention, but her hand phased right through him. Instantly, she started freaking out. She had no idea what was going on or what was coming next.

As Drake was just about to receive the Calzaniti Statue, an extremely large *Bang*, the largest ever, came from everywhere. Then just like that, Darkness came through the entrance of the arena, followed by Lord Taoî himself.

"No...."Jessica said to herself, then started running towards Drake. By the look of things, Drake was well prepared. As Lord Taoî approached Drake, he quickly held out the Calzaniti Statue towards Lord Taoî. Instantly, he started to disappear into the statue itself. Things were looking pretty positive when out of nowhere, Lance Jefferson appeared chanting some type of spell from a very old looking book. Jessica couldn't make out what Lance was chanting, but it definitely wasn't good. Just as Lance finished chanting, he immediately closed the book and a bright light appeared around Drake, nearly blinding almost everyone in the room. As soon as the light dissipated, Jessica looked down at where all of the action was and Drake had suddenly disappeared. What did Lord Taoî and Lance do to Drake was all Jessica could think about when everything went black again.

"Jessica? Jessica, are you okay?" Drake asked as he carefully shook Jessica's left arm. Just then, Jessica came back.

"What?" she asked, still somewhat out of it.

"Are you okay?" Drake re-asked.

"Yeah," she lied, "I'm fine."

"Are you sure?" Drake was somewhat worried at this point. Kim was also worried about her too.

"Yes guys, I'm perfectly fine," Jessica assured them. There was a brief moment of silence. "Hey, I have to go. I'll catch up with you two later," Jessica finally said then took off running and disappeared, leaving Drake and Kim very confused at what just happened.

As soon as Jessica got to her home, she started freaking out. She had no idea what had happened or what was going on.

"Jessica," came a calm voice from behind her. She immediately turned around, only to find Queen Evë standing behind her.

"Queen Evë? What's wrong?" Jessica asked with a bit of relief that it was Queen Evë.

"Come with me," she said as a portal to the Realm of Light appeared. Queen Evë held out her hand. Without any hesitation, Jessica grabbed her hand and the two entered the portal, closing immediately afterwards.

Chapter Eleven:

Stage Four

"Drake?" Zack asked, "what's wrong?"

"Hmm? Oh, yeah," Drake replied, focusing back to reality, "I just feel like there is something up with Jessica lately."

"Something bad... or dark?"

"Oh no!" Drake exclaimed, "....at least I hope not."

"Oshwaia," Jessica started to say.

"I know child," he interrupted her.

"But how?"

"Queen Evë and I converse now and then. She told me so I could watch over you."

"Thank you," Jessica said as she walked over to the door, "but I must be going now. Tomorrow is Stage Four and I know I need some rest."

"Goodnight," Oshwaia said as he nodded her goodnight.

"Goodnight Oshwaia," she said then left the room.

As Jessica left the temple, silence filled all around her. She slowly made her way to the living/housing level, heading to her home in Sector C-4. Walking home, the silence seemed almost eerie like to Jessica, which made her more on edge. Once at home, she stepped inside, shut the door, and began to walk away from it when all of a sudden, knocking came to her door. This really freaked her out. Fully prepared for anything, she answered the door.

"Drake?" she asked with relief in her voice.

"I'm sorry," he said, "is this a bad time?"

"What? Oh no! Come in! Come in!" she said, inviting him in.

"What happened today? Are you okay?" Drake asked as she closed the door. He was really concerned for her.

"Yeah, just wasn't feeling well was all," she lied to him, only to protect him.

"Oh, okay then," Drake told her as the two sat down. After spending some time with her to make sure she was truly alright, Drake headed off to pick up Zack then the two were off to the Training Room for some more training.

"Seriously Drake, what's wrong?" Zack asked as Drake kept losing his concentration.

"Huh? Oh," Drake stopped everything he was doing, "I just can't shake this off feeling about Jessica right now." Then, he continued punching the bag dangling in front of him.

"It's probably nothing," Zack replied.

"Yeah, you're probably right Zack," Drake agreed but boy, were they completely wrong.

"Here, try this," Zack said as he pulled out a bag with some weird looking fruit inside from Drake's belongings.

"What's that?" Drake asked as he stopped to see what Zack had.

"They're called matre berries," Zack answered, "Father Brai gave them to me to give to you."

"Do they do anything?"

"I.... I'm not sure," Zack thought about it for a moment, "I don't think he ever told me."

"It's okay," Drake said as he popped a berry into his mouth. He chewed for a moment, "it has an odd taste to it, but still tolerable." They laughed for a moment.

"So, how do you feel?" Zack finally asked.

"I…. I don't know," Drake replied, "normal I guess?" He punched the bag, which went flying across the room and into a wall, just barely sticking out. The two stood there, in shock. Drake barely moved towards the bag when he suddenly whooshed to it, in less than a second. Now, Drake and Zack were scared yet awed by the effects.

"I think Father Brai wants you to use these to get stronger," Zack said then gave Drake the bag of berries.

"I'm not sure," Drake replied as he took the bag, "thank you."

Zack yawned, "No problem. He paused, "well I'm beat and tomorrow morning is Stage Four. We should get some rest."

"Yeah. Go on ahead; I'll catch up," Drake said as they walked over to his belongings. Zack yawned again.

"Alright, see you shortly," Zack said then left the Training Room. Drake made sure Zack was completely gone and him completely alone before he ate a few more berries. He could feel the energy flowing through him. Instantly, he made four boulders appear from the rocks below him. One by one, he casted a spell and destroyed the boulders; a fireball, an iceball, a waterball, and another boulder, smaller in size. Drake's training had just become a whole new ballpark.

The next morning, even though he was extremely tired from all of the training the night before, Drake rolled himself out of bed. Without waking Zack up, he got ready for the next stage.

"Hey, you're awake," Zack yawned as he woke up and saw Drake.

"Yeah, woke up a little earlier and couldn't go back to sleep," Drake said. The two finished getting ready then headed out for another eventful day.

"Welcome! Welcome!" announced Oshwaia, "welcome to Stage Four contestants." The crowd cheered and roared. After calming the crowd down, he continued, "Father Brai will explain this level's rules." He took his seat while Father Brai took the podium.

"To be honest with you, "he started off as he spoke to the contestants, "I can only say out of the remaining forty-five contestants, the first thirty to make it back here to the arena will move on to Stage Five." Father Brai stepped back and as he did, Oshwaia stood up. The two switched places and Oshwaia took the podium.

"Contestants, as you head towards Stage Four's level, please pick up a map with a starting point on it. Then, wait for the signal and best of luck." Both the crowd and the contestants were confused now. What were Oshwaia and Father Brai up to?

"What do you think this stage will be about?" Jessica asked as Drake and herself each grabbed a map.

"I'm not sure," Drake replied, "but I guarantee you, it won't be easy."

Drake, Jessica, Lance, and the other forty-two contestants were all in position, waiting for the signal. A thousand thoughts were running through Drake's mind when the green luminäta suddenly went out. A few moments later, the red luminäta went out. Some contestants started freaking out. Then, the blue luminäta went out. Almost all of the contestants were freaking out by this point. The yellow luminäta was the last to go out and the closest one to Drake. All around him, contestants were freaking out but Drake was smarter than most of them. He figured out he has to make it to the center of the level and be one of the first thirty contestants to make it back. Feeling the walls for support, Drake started off, hoping to be going in the right direction. First a left, then another left, then a right, followed by yet another right. He had no idea where he was going but he knew he had past at least four contestants. Then, out of nowhere, two more contestants appeared, only to bump into each other and then a wall. Somehow, this amused Drake a little. He then started to think who else came up with a way to get to the arena. Was Jessica on her way or was she lost? What about Lance? After taking three more rights, Drake finally took a left then realized he was starting down a long hallway. Being very cautious and passing five or six contestants, Drake finally reached a crossroads; left or right? He first looked right, then left and only took a few steps to the left when *Bang* him and Jessica ran into each other accidentally.

"Oh my gosh, I'm so sorry! Are you okay?" Drake asked as he quickly got up to help Jessica up.

"Yeah I'm fine," she replied as she accepted his help, "what about you?"

"Yeah I think so," he replied.

"How many contestants do you think have made it back yet?" Jessica asked.

"To be honest with you, probably not many, but let's go together," Drake replied.

"And there are no rules about that."

"Nope," Drake replied, so the two decided to finish the stage together.

Meanwhile, Lance wasn't having as much good luck. When the green luminäta went out,

Lance started running in the direction he entered the room from. He barely entered anther room when the red luminäta went out. Lance kept running forward, right into a small pond in the middle of the room.

"Great," Lance said to himself as he quickly got out and shook off as much water as possible, hoping no one actually saw him fall. Suddenly, two more contestants fell into the same pond. Lance didn't feel so bad anymore. He quickly left the room, coming up to two hallways. Thinking he knew the way, Lance took the second hallway south, followed by a left and anther left. Then a dead end. Now pissed, he immediately turned around and darted back to the first hallway.

As Lance was making his way back, Drake and Jessica were continuing on.

"Look, I see a faint light that way!" Drake told Jessica as he pointed to the path north of them.

"Quickly!" she said. The two then ran for the light, finding the staircase heading up and down between the levels. They ran as fast as they could up the stairs.

As the two entered the Tessr Games Arena, the crowd was already cheering and roaring. The two barely made it, being the twenty-fifth and twenty-sixth contestants to make it back. Three more contestants came up behind the two, leaving only one spot to fill in order to move on. The crowd immediately quieted down to see who would be the last contestant to come up. Pure silence filled the room, then Lance came running into the arena. Simultaneously, the crowd broke out cheering and roaring.

After the remaining contestants were all accounted for, Oshwaia ended the stage.

"Give it up for the thirty contestants who will be moving on," he stated and the crowd cheered and roared. "I want to thank the contestants who will not be moving on, good job." The crowd cheered and roared again. After quieting the crowd down, Oshwaia finished, "That concludes Stage Four. Stage Five will be tomorrow so go, rest, and best of luck." The crowd cheered and roared a little. After the crowd started to break up, Drake was getting ready to leave when Lance stopped him.

"Congratulations Drake," he said as he stuck his hand out to shake with Drake.

"Oh hey, you too," Drake replied as he grabbed Lance's hand. As the two shook hands, Drake sensed something. The two then let go.

"Catch you tomorrow?" Lance asked, getting ready to leave.

"Yeah, see you tomorrow," Drake said. Lance walked away as Drake started to worry, because something was off about Lance and Drake had a feeling it wasn't good.

Chapter Twelve:

Stage Five

Stage Five was underway and the contestants had to find five objects, each a different color. Drake had just found his first item, a red ruby. Next on his list was a blue diamond. Drake hurried through the level, trying hard not to run into any other contestants. After what seemed like forever, Drake finally found the blue diamond he was searching for. Next, he had to look for a green emerald. As he started looking for one, the ruby and diamond started to glow in the direction of the third item. They grew brighter as he got closer until he entered another room. The two items stopped glowing.

"It must be somewhere in here," Drake said to himself. There were four contestants inside the room and another two were on their way in so Drake needed to hurry. After searching and searching, he was about to give up when out of the randomness he found his emerald. After finding the third item, Drake realized he found all three next to water. Was that just a coincidence or were his items truly located by water? He left the room to look for his fourth item when the three items started glowing, leading him towards the right direction.

"Look out!" shouted a contestant as she ran by Drake.

"Watch it!" shouted another as he nearly plowed Drake over. Being way more cautious, Drake entered yet another room. As he entered, the items stopped glowing, just as before. Item number four, a yellow gold bar had to be in that particular room. Surprisingly, it didn't take Drake long to find the gold bar.

"Four down, only one more to go," he told himself. He wondered how Jessica and Lance were doing, Jessica had three items and was searching for a red quartz crystal. Lance only had one item and was struggling to find a yellow opal. Drake then started wondering how many items other contestants had. Regaining focus on the task at hand, Drake took off for his final item, a silver fluorite. As before, his items pointed him in the direction he needed. However, when he entered the final room, the items didn't stop glowing. They started glowing brighter as he got closer to the water. Inside the water were hundreds of silver fluorites, but which one did Drake truly need? After going through at least fifty fluorites, Drake found a fluorite with the Tessr Games symbol carved into it.

"This has to be my final item," Drake said, out loud by accident. He quickly looked around but no one else was around him. He put the fluorite with the others, which finally stopped glowing. He finally had all five items. Drake ran as fast as he could towards the stairs back to the Tessr Games Arena until he ran into Jessica.

"Hey Drake," she said, somewhat surprising him.

"Oh, hey Jessica," he replied back.

"How many items do you have?"

"I have all five items. What about you?"

"Lucky! I just need my last one, a white moonstone."

"A white moonstone huh?" Drake asked, but as he asked, something strange happened. All five of Drake's items started glowing again. He held all five in his hands, trying to figure out what was going on. The glowing temporarily blinded Drake and Jessica. Then it suddenly stopped. After regaining sight, the two saw that there were no longer five items, but six now. Drake's sixth item was a white moonstone, the last item Jessica needed. Rather than being confused about what just happened, the two just accepted it and headed towards the arena.

Drake, Jessica, and Lance had all passed Stage Five, leaving only twenty-five contestants left. After quieting the crowd, Oshwaia ended the stage.

"Give it up for the twenty-five contestants moving on," he said and the crowd cheered and roared. "Let's also give it up for the contestants who will not be moving on, good job." The crowd cheered and roared more. After the crowd died down, Oshwaia finished speaking, "That concludes Stage Five. Stage Six will be in two days' time so go, rest, and best of luck." The crowd cheered and roared. Suddenly, Drake heard something; something from all the way from the surface. He looked around but no one else seemed to have heard it but him. He looked upwards. Whatever Lord Taoî was up to, it was only the beginning. Drake looked back down, only to find every single one of his friends staring at him, with concern and worry. Drake was just as concerned and worried as they were, but they were looking at him not only because he was 'The Chosen One', but for hope, which Drake had plenty of it to give.

Chapter Thirteen:
Darkness Is Lurking

With the Syclore, Kurëlzirlo, Rëptissh, and Gollunm now in place, Lord Taoî's plan was falling into place.

"Yes my lord?" Mariah asked as she bowed before Lord Taoî.

"Go to the Eastern Mountains and find the other entrance," he said, "we must breach all six of the entrances."

"Yes my lord," she replied then rose, "but why all six?"

"Because my little numoni," he paused, "in order for the Darkness and myself to get the one who can stop our plan entirely."

"You, you mean?"

"Indeed I do. Now go; time is of the essence," Lord Taoî demanded.

"Yes my lord," Mariah quickly bowed and left the room.

"Michael!" shouted Lord Taoî. Michael rushed into the room as quickly as he could.

"Yes my lord?" he asked as he bowed.

"I am giving you the same task. Go to the Vinn Forest and locate the final entrance," he ordered.

"Yes my lord," he replied and started to rise.

"But if you fail me," Lord Taoî started to say, catching Michael off guard and causing him to freeze in his place. Lord Taoî walked right up to him and got eye level with Michael.

"You won't see another day," he stated right in front of Michael. Lord Taoî could see the pure fear inside Michael's eyes, which caused him to chuckle for a moment. "Now go!" Immediately, Michael rose and darted out of the room.

As Michael, Christopher, and their men headed across the sea and into the Vinn Forest, Michael's "condition" had worsened and Christopher was becoming more worried for his leader.

"Michael?" Christopher started to ask, "whatever is happening to you is only getting worse. What's going on?" He cringed up, expecting a blow towards him; physically and verbally. But nothing happened. Michael and Christopher just continued ahead on their eglîmos with their men right behind them. They traveled a little deeper into the forest until Michael signaled them all to stop.

"Spread out and find that entrance!" he demanded. Immediately, everyone got off of their eglîmos, tied them up, and started looking for the entrance.

"Christopher? Follow me," Michael said as he started his search. The two looked in silence until Michael knew they were alone. He looked around to make sure they were truly one hundred percent alone before he started. "Christopher?" he asked.

"Yes?" he asked, somewhat scared. There was a brief moment of silence then Michael stopped looking and turned towards Christopher.

"Christopher," he started off, "I'm dying."

"Dying? What do you mean you're dying?" Christopher asked, shocked beyond belief. Michael lifted up his illro and several burn marks were growing all over his chest and stomach. Rapid sharp pains suddenly radiated from Michael's body, causing him to yell, but he didn't because he didn't want anyone else to know. A burn mark on Michael's left side grew with the pain. A new burn mark on the backside of his right leg appeared as well. "What happened? When did this start?" Christopher asked as Michael put his illro down.

"Shortly after Lord Taoî was released," Michael slowly stated as the pain subsided.

"Do you think he did this to you?"

"I don't know to be honest, but whoever created this curse is one powerful being" A group of leynolz swung high in the trees above, startling Michael and Christopher a little. Then the two went back to searching.

Meanwhile, Mariah wasn't having much luck either. After accidentally startling a herd of eccus and having a werzer pop out of nowhere,

Mariah was a little on edge. Stone after stone, tree after tree, Mariah kept looking for the entrance but was having no luck. She spent hours trying to find it but still no luck. Mariah knew she had to hurry for nightfall was coming up and Lord Taoî will be furious is she hadn't found it by then. Starting to panic, she started looking harder and faster.

As the Gollunm threw rock after rock, boulder after boulder, there was still no sign of the entrance as the beast destroyed everything in its path. Dusk was setting in and Lord Taoî was beyond inflamed.

"Day after day goes by and neither a single beast nor creature can find the bloody entrances," Lord Taoî snarled to himself, "might as well do it myself. I mean, even this stupid beast can't find an entrance." The Gollunm just continued to destroy, like Lord Taoî wasn't even there. Lord Taoî was just about to take things into his own hands when he sensed something near the Eastern Mountains. Pure Darkness appeared and consumed him. After it dissipated, he was gone.

Lord Taoî stepped out of the Pure Darkness that appeared, then it dissipated. Lord Taoî looked around at a hillside covered in fire, lava, and destruction. A pleased smile appeared on his face as he admired the Kurëlzirlo's work until it immediately vanished when he saw the Kurëlzirlo just standing there, not moving a single inch.

"What is wrong with you you stupid beast?" he demanded to know.

"Mmmaaasterrr," the Kurëlzirlo busted out as it pointed to a rocky spot that the lava seemed to be magically going around. A grin appeared on Lord Taoî's face.

"An entrance," he said, with a little delight in his voice. "Maybe you things aren't worthless after all," he told the Kurëlzirlo.

"Mmmaaasterrr," the beast cried out.

"Protect this entrance!" Lord Taoî ordered. The beast roared and obeyed. Pure Darkness reappeared to take Lord Taoî to his next destination.

Nightfall had just fallen and the moon was coming out, barely shining in the Realm of Darkness. Mariah was still frantically looking for the entrance. As she looked, she started to realize truly how much darker everything was in the Realm of Darkness. Panic started to turn into worry, which started to turn into loss of hope when something caught her eye. Off in the distance, a small twinkle appeared. After running towards it, the twinkle grew and became a doorway, encased in a faintly glowing magical spell.

"Well done," came Lord Taoî's voice from behind her. She immediately turned around.

"My lord, as you have asked," she said as she bowed to him.

"You have yet to disappoint me my little numoni," he stated.

"I will never fail you!" she replied back.

"We shall see. Now, protect this entrance!" he demanded.

"Yes my lord," she obeyed. Next, to see how Jewel City was holding up, if at all.

All of Jewel City was destroyed accept for four buildings; the racqutir's manor, the concert hall, the library, and the bazyra. Lord Taoî watched as the Syclore tried to destroy each building, but a magical spell protected them all.

"Trying to outsmart me 'Chosen One'?" Lord Taoî asked, amusing himself. He rose his left palm up, creating a ball of pure dark cosmic energy. Without even aiming, he released it on the concert hall. Piercing through a wall, the ball traveled to the center of the hall where an explosion occurred for only two seconds, immediately followed by an implosion for two seconds, immediately followed by remains turning to dust.

"That was easy," Lord Taoî laughed a little, "one down, three to go." He created another pure dark cosmic energy ball and aimed it at the racqutir's manor. He released the ball and the exact same thing happened to the manor as the concert hall. Which one was Lord Taoî going to destroy next? He created another pure dark cosmic energy ball and aimed it at the library. When he released it, the ball did not fly towards the library, but towards the bazyra. Once there, the ball exploded for two seconds, then imploded for two seconds, immediately followed by what remained turning to dust.

"Bingo!" Lord Taoî said with delight as he stared at the library. Lord Taoî now had three of the six entrances in his grasp. Now to find the other three.

Just as Michael, Christopher, and their men were about to give up, one soldier saved everyone's souls from Lord Taoî's wrath.

"Hey, I think I found something!" he shouted from the distance. Michael and Christopher came running towards the soldier. He was standing in front of some old buildings.

"Fan out!" ordered Michael, "and find that entrance!", the men rushed in and started looking for the entrance. They searched and searched but still had no luck.

"Well?" came Lord Taoî's voice from behind Michael. He immediately turned around and bowed before his master. "Have you found the entrance yet?" Lord Taoî asked. Michael was just about to speak when a different soldier came running up to the two.

"My lord," he started as he bowed, "we found it."

"The entrance?" Lord Taoî asked, a little intrigued.

"Yes my lord."

"Show me!" he demanded. The soldier shot up and the three went to where the soldier found the entrance, shortly followed by Christopher. The soldier led the three of them to a staircase leading below the ruins. The stairs led them to a small room. Engraved into the floor was the Tërcerlin symbol.

"Protect this entrance!" Lord Taoî ordered Michael to stay.

"Yes my lord," Michael responded back.

"Four down, only two more entrances to go!" Lord Taoî stated with a hint of delight in his voice. Pure Darkness appeared and just like that, the two disappeared from the room.

Chapter Fourteen:

Stage Six

After another long and hard day of training, Drake nearly passed out several times while just showering alone.

"Drake, I think you're pushing yourself too hard," Zack told him, very concerned.

"Is it really THAT bad?" Drake asked.

"I think so."

"Oh, I hadn't even noticed. How about this? We still have one more day before Stage Six. Let's do something else besides training huh?" Drake asked.

"Okay!" Zack said as he shook his silver wolf tail in excitement. They both then let out huge yawns and knew it was time to hit the hay. Zack got up onto the foot of the bed and was instantly out cold. Drake got into bed and slowly started to pass out, but not to dream.

"Drake?" he heard his name being called, "Drake, is that you?"

"Jessica?" Drake turned around to find Jessica running up to him.

"What's going on?" she asked.

"I'm not quite sure," Drake responded, "but I'm not liking this." Suddenly, everything became super bright, nearly blinding the two. Then, it subsided and Drake and Jessica gained their eyesight back. As the two looked around, they found themselves at the beginning of Stage Six.

"Welcome! Welcome!" Oshwaia shouted and the crowd immediately calmed down, "contestants, welcome to Stage Six. For this stage, each of you will be asked six different icromosses.

The first fifteen contestants to answer all six correctly and return back here will move onto Stage Seven. As you enter the stage, you will be handed a scroll on which will have your first icromoss's location," he paused for a moment, "wait for the signal and best of luck."

"What's going on Drake? This is starting to creep me out," Jessica said nervously.

"I don't know," he replied, getting a little nervous himself. Then, the two started fading into darkness from each other.

"Drake?" was all Jessica could say before she disappeared. Drake was now all alone; alone in the darkness. It seemed like hours had gone by when a faint light appeared in the distance. As Drake got closer to it, it got brighter. Before he knew it, the light was so bright it nearly blinded him. He quickly shut his eyes and started rubbing the brightness out. When things came into focus, things really got weird. Drake looked around, only to find himself in his bed and Zack at the bottom of it, still passed out. Things seemed a bit brighter than usual so it must have been early morning already. Drake got up as quietly as possible, trying hard to not wake up Zack. He got ready for the day and was attempting to leave when he opened his door to leave and Jessica was standing there, about to start knocking.

"Hey Jessica," he said quietly as he exited his home and closed the door behind him. "What are you doing here so early?" he asked her quietly.

"I need to speak with you urgently," she also spoke quietly, "come with me." She then turned around and started walking away. Drake followed. She took Drake to the very top of the temple inside the Labyrinth of the Archaics. They were in the same area when they noticed the hyîdrai attacking. The pockets of light were barely shining but still enough to see the temple's beauty as well as everything else.

"Drake, you trust me don't you?" Jessica asked as the two sat down, staring out into the labyrinth below.

"Of course I do. Why would you ever ask me a question like that?" Drake responded.

"I don't know….," she paused a moment. "Last night I had this crazy dream, and you were there too," she continued. Drake was about to tell her what he saw from the night before but Jessica started speaking again. "I think I'm going crazy…. or worse…."

"Worse?" Drake asked, starting to become worried.

"You know…. turn towards Darkness," she responded.

"Jessica!" Drake snapped, "You have WAY too much goodness inside of you to ever turn towards Darkness. You're kind and sweet and beyond caring."

"You really think so?" she asked, trying not to blush.

"Yes. Yes I do!"

"Thanks Drake," Jessica said as the two hugged each other. She then took a giant sigh of relief. It seemed so peaceful on top of the temple. The two sat there, staring into the labyrinth below. Drake suddenly felt something, something he's never experienced before. Was he starting to grow feelings for Jessica? Did she feel the same way? Suddenly, the thought of Zack popped inside Drake's head.

"Hey, I gotta go. I promised Zack we would hang out today," Drake said as he got up.

"Oh cool! I think I'm going to train for a while," Jessica responded as Drake helped her up. Thank you."

"You're welcome," Drake said. Then, the two headed back. Drake and Jessica got back down to the living/housing level, and split from there. Jessica headed over to Kim's house to see if she was awake yet while Drake headed home to see if Zack was up yet. As he got home, he quietly entered, trying hard not to wake Zack. He slowly closed the door.

"Drake!" Zack shouted, nearly causing Drake to jump through the roof. Zack had nearly scared Drake half to death. The two just laughed about it. "Where were you?" Zack asked as Drake joined him in the kitchen area for breakfast.

"Oh, Jessica just had a few quick things to talk about," Drake stated as he began to prepare homookl.

"Oooh, like whaaaaat? Zack asked, acting as though Drake and Jessica were together together.

"Oh, just nervous about the second half of the Tessr Games," Drake lied, but is wasn't Jessica who was truly nervous about the second half of the games. Drake knew the second half was going to be harder.

"Oh," Zack sighed, "okay." Drake finished making their hamookls and the two ate in silence.

"So what are we doing today Zack?" Drake asked as he finished cleaning up breakfast.

"I get to choose?" Zack asked surprisingly.

"Sure, why not," Drake replied. This made Zack extremely happy that he started hopping around. "Alright, calm down a little," Drake laughed as Zack accidentally ran into him. The two laughed a bit then finished getting ready for the day. As soon as Drake and Zack were outside their home, something seemed off. The two were about to leave Sector E when they noticed someone wearing a black cloak and hood sneaking around.

"Let's follow," suggested Zack.

"I'm right behind you," agreed Drake. The two followed closely behind the hooded person, trying to figure out who it was and where they were heading. At the very end of Sector E, the person stopped, looked around to make sure he or she wasn't followed then pressed a stone into the wall further. Suddenly, a secret passage way opened up and the figure quickly entered. Drake and Zack were right behind, trying to enter before it closed. All three made it in safely. The hooded person kept going, still unaware that Drake and Zack were still following him or her. As the two followed, Drake couldn't help but to look around. He spotted a sign that read "Sector F". Drake had no idea there was a Sector F, but why was it hidden? The hooded person stopped in front of what looked like an old nonworking fountain. He looked around and out of the shadows in front of him, Lance slowly sneaked out and approached the hooded person.

"Do you have it?" Lance asked very softly and cautiously. The hooded person pulled out what looked like a book all wrapped up. Lance immediately grabbed it and unwrapped it. Sure enough, it was indeed a book but one that Drake had never seen before. Something about that book was catching Drake's attention, and it wasn't good. "Very good," Lance said with satisfaction. Lance then handed the hooded person a bag of helas. The two nodded at each other then went their separate ways. Drake didn't care about the hooded person anymore; he wanted to know what Lance was up to. Drake and Zack followed Lance through a secret underground tunnel which connected Sector F to Sector C. Once inside Sector C-6, Lance headed home.

"What do we do now?" Drake asked Zack, "wait to see what else Lance is up to or move on with our day?"

"What do you think?" Zack asked back.

"Let's wait a bit just in case," Drake said and Zack agreed so for a few hours, Drake and Zack watched to see if Lance were to leave again. But he didn't.

"Can we go? I'm getting bored," Zack stated, starting to become really bored and started to play with his own tail.

"Yeah, so am I," Drake replied, so the two left. For the rest of the day, the two just hung out at home, trying to figure out what that book was and what Lance wanted with it.

That night, Drake had issues falling asleep. He knew he had seen that book before but where and what did Lance want with it? After repeating the same few questions over and over again, Drake soon fell asleep.

     "Welcome! Welcome!" Oshwaia shouted and the crowd immediately calmed down, "contestants, welcome to Stage Six. For this stage, each of you will be asked six different icromosses. The first fifteen contestants to answer all six correctly and return back here will move onto Stage Seven. As you enter the stage, you will be handed a scroll on which will have your first icromoss's location," he paused for a moment, "wait for the signal and best of luck." The twenty-five contestants headed for the stage, each picking up their scroll on the way. As Drake grabbed his, he thought to himself how hard could this be? He was definitely about to find out.

When the last contestant got into place, they all waited for the signal....which never came. Drake started to become a little worried and concerned. Without even realizing it, he opened his scroll again. When he looked at it, it was no longer a map, but his first icromoss. It read:

> I am round and clear.
>
> I come in multiple sizes.
>
> I only have one purpose.
>
> What am I?

Drake thought about it for a moment when the memory of when him and Zack met Father Brai. He remembered when he teleported them to the Vinn Forest by space jumping.

"Space Jumping Sphere?" Drake asked out loud. Instantly, his scroll began to change. The words became a map, showing him where to go for his second icromoss. One down and five left to go.

Meanwhile, Jessica's first questing was a bit tougher:

> By day, I bring light.
>
> By night, I am out of sight.
>
> I am three into one.
>
> But really one into three.
>
> What am I?

Jessica thought really hard on it.

"The suns," she answered, but nothing happened. "The three suns?" she answered differently but still nothing happened. Her first question was stumping her and she was starting to get a little upset. After taking a deep breath, Jessica thought harder about her first question. She thought hard about each sun's name. "Sun Ti, Sun Ea, and Sun Rou?" she hesitated as she asked.

Instantly, her scroll began to change and she was off for icromoss number two.

> From deep within the
> Artumos-Craine.
> Came blood, fire, and hell
> from above.
> But finally defeated by the
> Book of Megi.
> Who am I?

This was Lance's second question as it appeared on his scroll once he had arrived at the right destination.

"That's easy," he said with a smile on his face, "Gruîd Almighty." Instantly, the scroll change and revealed his third question.

As Drake hurried to his third icromoss, he couldn't help but to laugh at his last one. I am calmer towards the center, but more chaotic around the edges. What am I? For Drake, the answer was so simple and easy; a storm. He laughed again. As he approached the spot on the scroll, his third icromoss appeared:

> At the beginning of life,
>
> I use four legs.
>
> Halfway through,
>
> I use two legs.
>
> At the end pf the journey,
>
> I use three legs.
>
> What am I?

Drake thought and thought about this question, and thought about it some more. Nothing was coming to him, no answer that would answer his question. Was this it? Was he done for?

Suddenly, an idea just popped into Drake's head and he immediately blurted it out.

"A living person?" he cautiously asked. Instantaneously, the icromoss changed to his fourth location and without any hesitation, he darted for the area urgently.

Once at his fourth location, Drake took a moment to catch his breath. Once calm, he read his fourth icromoss:

> I am located near a vast
> amount of water.
> I am as bright as a crystal.
> But my four walls protect me
> so.
> What am I?

"I'm as bright as a crystal, protected by four walls, and located near a vast amount of water," Drake said, trying to figure out the icromoss. He thought really hard about the question but only for a brief moment. Suddenly, the answer just came to him. "Jewel City," he answered. Just like before, the scroll changed and revealed his fifth location, which wasn't far from his current.

Once at her fourth location, Jessica read her next icromoss:

> Between mountain and fire.
>
> And on a plain of blue.
>
> My waters are pure.
>
> And with magical properties
>
> too.
>
> What am I?

Thought after thought after thought. Idea after idea after idea. Nothing was coming to mind. She started freaking out because only fifteen contestants were moving on and she had no idea how many were done with their icromosses. After taking a deep breath, she tried to come up with the right answer.

"Water that is pure and magical," Jessica said. "Pure and magical," she repeated. She took a moment to think. "Between mountain and fire, and on a plain of blue." She thought more. "Plain of blue, plain of blue…. Well pure and magical water comes from springs, but mountain, fire, plain of blue….wait….," she paused, "The Perzina Springs?" she answered, hoping to be right. Turns out she was right as her scroll changed to her fifth location. "Thank god!" Jessica said with relief than took off again.

Drake quickly read his fifth icromoss:
    It is redder than red.
    And bluer than blue.
    It gives good luck.

But only for two.

What am I?

Drake thought about it, "redder than red, bluer than blue, good luck but only for two...." He pondered about it until he remembered learning about something of that nature in pinquainta. He remembered learning about different crystals and how only one kind of them gives good luck.

"The Urmcrie Necklace?" Drake guessed. Suddenly, his scroll changed, showing his sixth and final icromoss location. Once at his location, the icromoss appeared. It was the toughest one of them all and Drake was in for a fun time answering:

I am fast but I am slow.

I am big but I am small.

I am many but I am few.

What am I?

Drake did not have the slightest clue. He thought long and hard about his final icromoss but nothing was coming to mind. He started guessing, "eglîmo." Nothing happened. "Eccu? Leynolz? Vemqur?" he asked but still nothing happened. Drake had absolutely no idea and started to worry. Had anyone completely answered all of their icromosses yet? Was he the only one on his final icromoss? A lot of questions started popping in his head, making him become distracted. He cleared his mind to focus on his final icromoss, and his finally icromoss only. He thought and thought and thought and still no answer.

"You," came Queen Evë's voice. Drake immediately looked around but he was still alone. "You," came her voice again. Drake had not seen nor heard from Queen Evë in a long time so he was very happy to hear her voice, knowing she was at least still alive.

"Me?" Drake responded back, not understanding what she was meaning.

"You," Queen Evë said again.

"Me….me….me….," Drake was trying hard to get her reference. He decided to start naming other "me" words, "Me………. umm……. I……. ughh….. myself?" Instantly, Drake's scroll started to glow. The light nearly blinded him, causing him to drop the scroll. The moment it hit the ground, it immediately stopped glowing, like a flip of a switch. After regaining his eyesight, he picked up his scroll and looked at it. It was showing him to head back to the Tessr Games Arena. At that moment, Drake realized he had just completed all six of his icromosses and darted for the arena.

Just before Drake entered the arena, an eerie silence came from the entrance. With a lot of caution, he slowly entered the arena. Once inside, the silent crowd busted into cheers and roars. He was the very first contestant to complete Stage Six. Shortly after more contestants started arriving at the arena. Jessica was the fourth contestant to move on and lance was the ninth. Before they knew it, they had their fifteen contestants moving onto Stage Seven.

"Give it up for the fifteen contestants moving on," Oshwaia said as the crowd cheered and roared, "and for the ten contestants who won't be moving on." The crowd cheered and roared even more. After quieting them down, Oshwaia finished up Stage Six, "that concludes Stage Six. Stage Seven will be held tomorrow morning so go, rest, and best of luck." The crowd then broke up and Drake's day finally came to an end.

Chapter Fifteen:

Escape From Darkness

"Hello and welcome to Stage Seven," Father Sage stated, then the crowd busted into cheers and roars. Drake was a little confused. For the past six stages, Oshwaia opened and closed each stage, but for this one he was nowhere in sight. So where was he? Drake looked around the entire arena but still saw no sign of Oshwaia. The crowd calmed and Father Sage continued, "to begin with, Oshwaia is feeling a little under the weather today so he will not be joining us." He paused a moment, "now, for Stage Seven. In this stage, you will only have one goal; do not fall. The first five contestants to fall will not be moving onto Stage Eight. I wish you all the best of luck and have fun!" Then, the crowd cheered and roared as the remaining fifteen contestants headed down to Stage Seven.

Once on level seven of the labyrinth, everyone headed north to the starting point. Inside a large room, sand covered most of the floor while thick jotrei hung from above. Once all fifteen contestants were inside the room, a large rumbling sound came from out of nowhere. Suddenly, the sand started to turn into water, rushing and flowing everywhere.

"Grab the jotrei," came Queen Evë's voice from inside Drake's head. Without any hesitation, he did exactly what he was told to do and the other contestants followed. The water rushed around Drake, nearly causing him to let go but luckily he didn't. However, the current was too strong and two contestants were swept from their spots. Now,

Drake just had to wait for three more contestants to fall and he would be moving onto Stage Eight. After about a minute of hanging in water, another large rumble came from nowhere. Then, all of the water started flowing to the far west wall. The water slowly climbed the wall and before everyone knew it, all of the water was now all up against the wall. Without warning, the water leaped off the wall, turning into wind. Holding on tightly, the contestants waited for the wind. At first it wasn't that strong until it started to pick up. Still holding on, no contestants fell. The wind picked up again and started blowing in all directions. Sadly, one contestant could not hold on. When he fell, a gust of wind caught him and carefully landed him to the ground. Three down, two to go.

Another rumble came and the wind instantly changed into falling snow; constant falling snow. The temperature started dropping. Everyone left got really cold. Within minutes, Drake could see his own breath. A few contestants, including Jessica started to shiver until another contestant fell. Luckily, she fell onto a pile of snow. Only one more contestant to fall and hopefully Drake and Jessica would move on. Yet another rumble came and the snow stopped. The temperature stopped dropping too but then started climbing upward to room temperature. The shivering came to a stop as the temperature started rising again. Slowly, sweat accumulated on everyone and they had begun to grow weak and tired. Only one more contestant needed to fall. One by one, it seemed like each contestant was getting weaker and weaker. A few contestants started losing their grips, including Lance. Suddenly, a contestant started to pass out, causing him to fall. The contestant didn't fall far so it barely hurt. Then, the temperature dramatically fell back to room temperature and the stage was over.

"Let's give it up for the ten contestants moving onto Stage Eight," Father Sage stated and the crowd cheered and roared. "And let's give it up for the five contestants who won't be moving on," he continued and the crowd cheered and roared more. Shortly afterwards, the crowd quieted down and Father Sage ended the stage. "This ends Stage Seven. In two days, we will host Stage Eight. Get plenty of rest, heal up, and best of luck in Stage Eight."

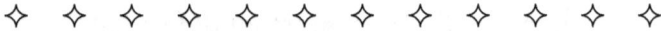

When the night fell each night, it seemed nearly pitch black. Doreen cuddled into Steven's arms as close as she could to feel even the slightest bit safe. One night, no one was in the room with Doreen, Steven, and Father Izea. Doreen and Steven were curled up together while Father Izea paced the cell, trying to find a way out. Something just outside the cell caught his attention. He couldn't quite tell what it was but definitely something silver. He walked over to it, reached out, and picked it up off of the ground. Turns out, he just found a cell door key, but did it belong to their cell? Trying to put the key into the lock, the noise woke up the Shaw's.

"What are you doing Father Izea?" Doreen asked fearfully.

"I found a key so I'm trying to escape," he replied quietly.

"Stop!" demanded Steven, "or you are going to get us ki…." Steven was interrupted by a *click* noise. Father Izea pulled the key back, pushed on the door, and watched it open. Doreen and Steven shot up.

"Look, do you want to get out of here or not?" Father Izea persisted. Doreen looked at Steven with very little hope left and they both knew exactly what to do.

"Let's go," Steven said as the two got up and headed over to the door. The three slowly crept their way through the other cells until they came to an actual door. "The way out?" Steven suggested.

"Quite possibly," Father Izea replied. Very cautiously, he slowly opened the door. Luckily, they were correct and they slowly inched outside. There was a little bit more light outside which made seeing easier, but they only saw one or two guards.

"Where is everyone?" Father Izea quietly asked as they headed towards the edge of the city.

"Looking for the labyrinth's entrances," came a voice from behind them. The three immediately jolted around to find one of Christopher Anders' soldiers behind them. Immediately, they rose their arms and surrendered. "Please, please," he stated softly, "I'm not here to harm you or take you back in." This information completely surprised the three. "I'm actually here to help you." That shocked Doreen, Steven, and Father Izea so much that Doreen almost fainted.

"Why? Why would you want to help us?" Steven asked the soldier.

"I'm done serving Christopher Anders, I'm done serving Michael Cashner, but above all else I'm done serving Lord Taoî! All they want is nothing but destruction, chaos, and darkness. I," he started to say when *Beep.... Beep.... Beep....* an alarm started going off, *Beep.... Beep.... Beep....* "They know you have escaped. Quickly, follow me!" the soldier stated then took off running. Without hesitation, Doreen and Steven began to follow him until Father Izea grabbed Steven's arm.

"Are you sure this is a good idea? Can we even trust him?" he asked.

"What other choice do we have? Now let's go!" Steven answered. He pulled away and took off running, with Father Izea right behind.

Just outside Moonshiar, the four paused to catch their breaths for a moment.

"Is everyone alright? Anyone hurt?" the soldier asked.

"No, I think we are all fine, thank you," Steven replied. The soldier took off his headgear.

"Good," he said as he extended his arm, "my name is Andrew Ree."

"My name is Steven Shaw," Steven said as he shook Andrew's hand, "and this is my lovely wife, Doreen."

"Pleasure," she said as she shook his hand as well.

"The pleasure is all mine," Andrew responded.

"And I am Father Izea," Father Izea introduced himself as the two shook hands. Silence fell around them as they thought they were out of the clear until....

"Run!" Andrew shouted as he spotted a horde of oxxtrades heading right for them. The four immediately took off towards the beach. Once at the beach, dolluus started flying in from nowhere.

"Look out!" Steven shouted as the dolluus darted down towards them.

"Quickly, this way!" Andrew shouted as he hurried for a faau he spotted in the distance. The four quickly boarded and took off as fast as they could. The dolluu flew above them but stopped attacking while the oxxtrades stopped at the shoreline. The dolluu landed next to the oxxtrades as the group got further out to sea. The show was now on the horizon when out of nowhere two fins appeared. Starting to circle the boat, two more fins appeared. By this time, Andrew and Steven had managed to find an emergency lifeboat to try to escape since the boat itself started to rotate in the same direction as the fins. Andrew ran to the edge and peered out at the fins.

"Rulooms!" he shouted, "to the lifeboat NOW!" The four ran as fast as they could to the lifeboat as the fins and water rotated faster and faster, starting to cause a funnel with them directly in the center. Doreen and Steven made it to the lifeboat and Andrew was almost there when an octopus-like arm flew from the waters, hitting the side of the faau, shoving it out of the rotating waters. Suddenly a naeinzira appeared, retracting its arm back. This angered the Rulooms, causing two of them to guard the faau while the other two attacked the naeinzira. Like hitting a ball with a baseball bat, the naeinzira took an arm and hit a ruloom causing it to fly out of the waters, over the faau, and crashing into the waters in the distance. It suddenly became war between the rulooms and the naeinzira and the four were caught in the mists of it all. They all got to the lifeboat safely and just in time because one of the naeinzira's arms struck the front of the faau, completely destroying it and causing the faau to begin taking water.

"We need to leave NOW!" shouted Doreen in fear of dying. All three men pushed and pushed but the lifeboat wouldn't budge. They tried again until a ruloom crashed into the side of the faau, right next to where they were. They instantly froze but one of the naeinzira's arms grabbed the ruloom and pulled it away. The faau was taking in more water and was definitely sinking and fast. Circumstances looked dire but the second crash loosened up the lifeboat. Going faster than ever, the four hurried with the lifeboat. They started it up and were able to exit the faau unnoticed. They were getting farther away when suddenly, Pure Darkness appeared in front and above them. Lord Taoî emerged from within the Pure Darkness.

"What is the meaning of this?" he spoke to his beloved beasts. Instantly, they stopped fighting and bowed to their master. Looking down at them, he noticed something floating in the water. As he reached down to pick it up, it caused a wave that pushed the four directly under Lord Taoî and past him, managing to complete their escape. Once he had the object in this hand, he realized it was one of Christopher Ander's faaus. He crushed it completely in his hand and then released it. "My pets," he started to speak as he rose back up. Suddenly, the oxxtrade came swimming in while the dolluu came flying. Both stopped next to the rulooms and the naeinzira. "Our prisoners have escaped due to a numoni. Find them and find them now!" he ordered. Without a single hesitation, all of his beasts immediately started fanning out, looking for the escapees. Pure Darkness appeared again and Lord Taoî went back to looking for the last two entrances.

A very small island appeared ahead of the four, who instantly decided to stop there. Once on shore, they buried the lifeboat.

"Look, a trapdoor?" shouted Steven as he stumbled upon what looked like a trapped door. In the distance, a few oxxtrade and dolluu were headed their way.

"Quickly!" Father Izea whispered as he pointed out the incoming danger. First, Father Izea headed down the trapdoor followed by Doreen, then Steven, and lastly Andrew. Just as Andrew shut the trapdoor, it locked and produced its own cloaking spell, completely hiding them from the beasts above.

Chapter Sixteen:

Stage Eight

The day before Stage Eight, Zack was peacefully resting, Jessica and Kim were doing a little training, and Lance was just chilling outside his home. But where was Drake?

"Thank you for coming Drake," Oshwaia said as the two journeyed into the temple further.

"It sounded urgent," Drake stated.

"It could be," Oshwaia replied then stopped at a door, "do you remember what Father Brai said about us helping you?"

"I do," Drake replied uncertain of where Oshwaia was going with this.

"What I am about to show you won't help you win, but it will help you succeed."

"Okay?" Drake was now confused. Oshwaia then opened the door and stepped into the room and Drake followed. Once inside, Oshwaia quickly closed the door, locked it, and lit the room.

"What....what are those?" Drake asked as he looked at what appeared to be blueprints to creating a creature, like Father Izea did. Oshwaia walked passed Drake to the far end of the room and flipped a switch. Other lights turned on, revealing cages with several creatures in each cage, one hundred percent like the creatures in the blueprints.

"Father Mika created them for the next stage," Oshwaia finally answered Drake, "we call them aameritz."

"Aameritz?" he repeated, trying to pronounce it correctly. Drake looked closely at them, almost examining them. "You said they were for Stage Eight?" he asked.

"Yes," was all Oshwaia could say. This really made Drake start thinking.

"Where are we?" Doreen asked.

"I'm not sure," Steven answered while trying to comfort her.

"Let's keep going!" Andrew insisted. The four started down a long hallway. Soon, the hallway shifted northwest and what seemed like forever, they came to a giant door. The amount of cobwebs and dust had shown the door hadn't been touched in years. Several torches were lit along the doorframe, giving light and showing a horrifying beast carved into the door. Around the beast was what looked like an ancient language.

"Father Izea? Can you read this?" Andrew asked as he studied the words.

"I, I think so," Father Izea stated as he approached the door. He studied the words carefully for a moment. "Baqu te bese cotu, que dipto konte wzer," Father Izea froze.

"Well?" Steven finally asked, "what does it say?"

"Beware the beast inside, for death lays ahead," he translated.

"Let's go back," Steven stated nervously.

"I agree," Doreen chimed in. Before anyone else could move or say another word....

"Eeeeennntteeerrrrrr!" rang an eerie voice form nowhere then suddenly, the giant door opened. The four started to step back when a force sucked them into the room, closing the door behind them.

"It won't budge!" exclaimed Steven as he tried to open the door, but it wouldn't move. Andrew and Father Izea joined but still no luck.

"Now what?" Doreen asked, shaking a little from fear. Steven wrapped his arms around his wife to comfort her and the four of them slowly turned around. They glanced around the room, looking for whoever or whatever called for them. Nothing. It was a completely empty room, or so they began to think. Andrew quickly pulled out his sword, ready for anything. He slowly started walking forward, followed by the Shaw's, and lastly Father Izea in the rear. They very quietly and carefully crept toward the center of the room. At that point, the tip of an end of a very large snakelike beast fell just to the far right of Andrew. It fell clockwise around the group. As it fell, it got larger until it reached Andrew again. A body fell directly in front of him. Scoping up the body, the four froze as they looked upon a four armed snakelike beast with two heads, one for chaos and the other for destruction. Their eyes were as black as pitch black could be. The beast's heads screeched simultaneously, causing everyone to cover their ears. While being distracted, the beast flung its tail at our hero's feet, tripping them right where they stood. Andrew quickly got up.

"Go!" he shouted as he started swinging his sword at the beast. The other three quickly got up and started running for the giant door. Doreen and Steven took off first, followed by Father Izea until the beast struck him with his tail causing him to go flying into a wall. "Hey!" Andrew shouted, trying to distract the beast, "hey! Over here you ugly thing!" Upsetting the beast, it focused all of its destruction on Andrew.

"Father Izea, are you alright?" Doreen asked as her Steven came running to him.

"Yeah," he slowly said as he picked himself up. At that exact moment, Andrew had managed to cut the beast twice and completely cut off one arm.

The beast was furious, going after Andrew with everything it had. Andrew kept dodging the blows and swinging his sword. Several more cuts were made and two more arms came off. Beyond livid, the beast attacked Andrew which caused him to drop his sword. The beast swung its tail at him, throwing him across the room and into a wall, but much harder than Father Izea. The throw was so hard, Andrew's body made a small indent in the wall.

"Andrew!" shouted the Shaw's, as they hurried over to help him. The beast immediately darted towards Andrew. Father Izea knew Andrew was toast unless he did something and quick. Father Izea took off as fast as he could towards Andrew's sword. Once in his hands, he threw it towards the beast. The sword struck the beast in the chest, pinning it to the wall.

"Chi ma cata de louw!" Father Izea shouted once the beast realized it wasn't going anywhere. Ice shot from Father Izea's palms. The ice struck the beast and as it struck, it began freezing the beast. The beast was only halfway frozen when Father Izea stopped and fell due to exhaustion. The ice just kept continuing to freeze the beast. Breathing heavily, Father Izea rose and headed over towards the sword. He grabbed the sword and carefully pulled it out, cautiously so he wouldn't break the ice around it. Once the sword was back in his hands, he walked up to the beast's heads, which were now being covered with ice. Once the heads were covered, the entire beast would be completely frozen. With a swing of Andrew's sword, Father Izea swung in the direction of the two heads. Completely shattering the two heads off the body, Father Izea had saved them all. The heads hit the ground, shattering into pieces.

Shortly afterwards, the rest of the body shattered like the heads. Father Izea then slowly made his way to the others.

"Not bad," Andrew slowly said to Father Izea. Silence filled the room.

"Not bad yourself," he finally replied back. The two stared at each other for a moment then both started laughing, followed by the Shaw's. As the four laughed, the now dead beast turned into a cloud of darkness. The four instantly stopped laughing and watched as the dark cloud spiraled upwards. It spun in the air for only a moment, then like a snake, it slivered to a corner of the room and disappeared through it. The giant door reopened and the four were now safe.

Drake looked down at the labyrinth below. Izmorais kept the area lit for him to see. He had come a long ways in the games but he still had three more stages to complete. Things were definitely getting more intense and Drake still couldn't figure out the next stage. He finally decided to call it a night and headed off to get some rest before Stage Eight. That next morning, Drake met up with Jessica on the way to Stage Eight.

"Morning Jessica," he said as he came running up behind her.

"Oh, morning Drake," she responded back, "ready for this stage?"

"No." Then the two laughed as they got closer to the arena. "Well," Drake started to say. "seven down, three to go." Saying this caused the two to laugh again. Before they knew it, they were in front of the Tessr Games Arena's entrance.

"Good luck today Drake!" Jessica wished Drake good luck.

"Thanks, good luck to you too!" he wished her good luck back and the two entered the arena.

"Welcome! Welcome!" Oshwaia announced and the crowd began to quiet down, "contestants, welcome to Stage Eight." He paused and waited for the crowd to silence itself. Once quieted, Oshwaia continued, "the task for this stage is very simple; avoid being caught by the aameritz." The crowd and contestants looked at each other with puzzled looks. Only Drake, Father Mika, and Oshwaia knew what the aameritz were. "The first five contestants to get caught by the aameritz will not move onto Stage Nine," Oshwaia continued, "as you enter the stage, you will be handed a scroll on which is your starting location." He paused for a moment, "wait for the signal and…." Before Oshwaia could continue, a snakelike cloud of darkness appeared from the center of the ceiling. It circled the arena, causing people to start to panic. Without any hesitation, Drake closed his eyes and aimed his hands in the air.

He then took a deep breath, opened his eyes, and shouted, "Chi ma cata de louw!" Ice shot from Drake's palms, aimed right at the circling dark cloud. It struck the cloud, turning it to ice and freezing it to the ceiling. Once it was three-fourths of the way frozen, Drake stopped. He nearly fell from exhaustion, but a few other contestants helped by catching him. The cloud continued to freeze all the way around. Once it was completely frozen, it shattered and disappeared. Everyone waited in silence to see if it would return, but it didn't. Everyone started cheering and roaring; everyone but Drake, Jessica, Lance, and Oshwaia. Drake had saved the day again but how did a cloud of darkness get in was all the four could think about at that moment.

Down where the aameritz were being kept waiting to be released, the very first aameritz, a little bigger and stronger than all the rest, started acting up. It started to yell and throw a fit when suddenly it stopped, and its eyes turned pure black; black as night.

Everyone waited to see if Stage Eight or even the Tessr Games itself would continue. After much consideration, Stage Eight commenced. The ten contestants remaining started to get into positions. Once ready, the stage began.

The cage doors opened to where the aameritz were, but none of them moved. Every aameritz's eyes were pure black.

"Go!" came Lord Taoî's voice speaking to the first aameritz, and the entire herd of them busted out and darted towards the level. Silence rang throughout the level until one scream shattered it. Then came another. Drake instantly knew something was wrong. He knew in his heart that Father Mika wouldn't make anything dark. The dark cloud; when it disappeared, it must have possessed the aameritz. Another scream rang out and Drake started off, hoping to find Jessica safe and unharmed. He got to the room where the last stage was held and there they were. Only a few aameritz were there when one looked in his direction. Drake noticed its eyes were pure black and before, they were green. Because of this,

Drake instantly knew he was right. The aameritz noticed Drake and gave out a rattling-like noise. This quickly caught the attention of the other aameritz in that area of the level and suddenly they were all after him. He ran as fast as he could towards the entrance. He heard three more screams in front of him as he ran, followed by the aameritz. He passed a hallway, immediately stopped, and hid right inside the hallway, hoping the aameritz would just continue forward. The creatures ran right passed him. A few moments later, another scream came from the same direction the creatures were heading; Jessica's screams.

Drake ran into a room filled with pillars of different sizes. He looked around, trying to find Jessica. He heard her screams again at the end of the room. He ran as fast as he could towards her. Once there, he found her caught up against one of the pillars. Without hesitation or even thinking, Drake shot a fireball at one of the aameritz. It instantly vaporized the creature into nothing, destroying the darkness within for good. One of the aameritz surrounding Jessica was the first one and killing one of its own really angered it. The creature let out a cry, signaling the other aameritz. Fireball after fireball and creature destroyed after creature destroyed, Drake was saving everyone again, including Jessica when suddenly the first aameritz grabbed her and started climbing up the closest pillar.

"Drake!" she shouted at him. As the creature climbed higher, more and more aameritz came flooding in, overwhelming him and piling on top of him. Jessica surely thought Drake was a goner. Suddenly, a bright red light started to shine in between the aameritz, where Drake was. Just like that, a snakelike ball of fire shot out, destroying every single aameritz in its path. The snakelike fireball destroyed every last aameritz, except for the one holding Jessica. Beyond angry, the first and now last aameritz dropped Jessica. She screamed as she fell. She abruptly stopped when Drake caught her. Drake and Jessica caught eye to eye for a moment. Something definitely sparked inside both of them. The last aameritz let out a loud rattling-like noise. It jumped off the pillar and was headed right for Drake. He quickly let Jessica down and prepared himself for the aameritz's attack. Jessica had barely gotten out of the way when the creature attacked Drake. The creature tried scratching, biting, and just in general attacking him.

From out of nowhere, Drake shouted, "Kabous tuis!" Several large size boulders broke loose from all around the three. They circled high above Drake and the creature. Catching it off guard, Drake was able to throw the creature high into the sky. Once it was in the exact center of the flying boulders, they came crashing inwards, destroying the last aameritz and the darkness for good. The boulders then flew back to where they came from. Drake suddenly dropped to his knees and Jessica came running to him.

"Are you alright?" She asked as she helped him back up.

"Yeah, I think so," he replied.

"What just happened?"

"I…. I don't know." Drake knew something was definitely going on and Darkness was finally coming.

"In light of the recent turn of events, I hereby declare that all ten contestants will move onto Stage Nine," Oshwaia stated. Most of the crowd cheered and roared but some were a little scared and frightened. "This concludes Stage Eight. Stage Nine will be in two days so go, rest, and best of luck." The crowd cheered and roared. Both Drake and Oshwaia knew at that moment that something bigger than they expected was coming.

Chapter Seventeen:
Drake's First Kiss

That evening after Stage Eight, Jessica spent a little time over at Kim's house. As the luminätas began to glow brighter for nighttime, Jessica started her trip home. Once there, she saw a note attached to her door. Confused, she slowly opened it and read it:

> Temple of the Archaics,
>
> Northern Gate,
>
> Tomorrow Afternoon.
>
> D.S.

"D.S.?" she thought to herself, "who could that be? Drake maybe?" There was no sense of danger when she read it. After much consideration, she finally decided to go check out whoever this D.S. was.

Lance hurried his way through Sector F-1 and F-2. He even ran completely through F-3. Hidden behind Sector F-3 was a single building that looked like it was attacked, the halfway destroyed building was a great place for Lance to go. He paused to make sure he was truly alone then entered the slowly crumbling building. He went to about the center of the building and pulled out the same book Drake and Zack saw him receive. He stared at it for a moment, opened it, and flipped through some pages. He stopped on a certain page.

"Vergree su trui darkness," he read out loud and then closed the book. He pulled out a sphere and waited. He waited and waited but nothing happened. Suddenly, a cloud of darkness appeared above him. "There you are," he stated as the cloud circled about him. Without any hesitation, Lance quickly trapped the cloud inside the sphere. Using a form of dark magic, he summoned a picture of Lord Taoî's head inside the sphere.

"Who are you.... numoni?" Lord Taoî spoke to Lance.

A little nervous, Lance finally spoke, "my name is Lance Jefferson my lord and I'm here to serve you." Silence fell over the two for a brief moment until Lord Taoî started laughing.

"And what makes you think you can just start serving....," Lord Taoî started to say but abruptly stopped when he glimpsed the book behind Lance. "What....what is that behind you?" he asked.

"What, this old thing?" Lance asked as he grabbed the book and showed Lord Taoî. For the first time since before he was trapped inside The Ancient Five, fear came across his face.

"The Book of Megi," he slowly stated. Silence quickly filled the room. Shortly after, Lord Taoî began to smile. "Tell me, Lance," Lord Taoî started off, "which side do YOU choose?"

"I will always choose you and Darkness, my lord," Lance said as he bowed to the image.

"Good," Lord Taoî said, "good." There was a brief moment of silence. "Having someone on the inside really sets my plan into action," Lord Taoî finally spoke, "your first task is do not let anyone know you have that book, especially 'The Chosen One'. If he gets that book, everything I've been doing falls apart and my plan will be ruined."

"May I ask what your plan is?" Lance hesitantly asked.

"To take over everything," Lord Taoî stated, "and now, I have someone on the inside to really help get my plan moving."

"What can I do to help my lord?" Lance asked as he bowed to his master.

"Find all of the labyrinth entrance's and destroy all of the protection spells on them." Then the two started laughing evil laughs.

Throughout the day, Jessica asked every hiumän she came in contact with if he or she knew a D.S. Most only knew D.S. to possibly be Drake Shaw and others had no idea. But what would Drake want at the northern gate? Did he want to do some training there? With lots of questions on her mind, Jessica started her journey to the gate.

Once there, she found a trail of zeqtouras leading to the temple. This made Jessica very confused. She picked one up. It was her favorite color and scent; violet and lavender. D.S. had to have been Drake because very few knew her favorite color let alone her favorite scent. Holding the zeqtoura still, Jessica started following the trail. She followed the zeqtouras into and through the temple. Then, the trail stopped in front of a closed door. She slowly opened the door and stepped into a room. The room was covered in lit zeqtouras. Jessica was so confused at what was going on. She closed the door and looked around. On the opposite side of the door was a doorway leading to a balcony. Once out there, at the edge of the balcony was Drake looking out over the labyrinth below.

"Drake, is that you?" Jessica asked as she slowly approached him. He did not answer but instead turned around with a smile on his face.

"Thank you for coming," he replied.

"Of course," she answered, "but why am I here? What is all of this?" She pointed to all of the zeqtouras around them. Drake grabbed her hands and took her to a table he had prepared himself. He had prepared a full meal for the two of them, hoping she would say yes to him.

"You made dinner?" she asked, shocked.

"Well, I tried to," he jokingly replied.

"Well it looks and smells delicious!"

"Really?"

"Really really!"

"Would you like to try some?" he asked, a little hesitant.

"I'd love to!" she shouted with excitement. So they spent the next hour or so trying the delicious meal Drake had prepared for them. Afterwards, the two started talking about their pasts; how Jessica truly became blind, how Drake first learned to play esocro, and even how he had never even kissed someone before.

"Are you serious?" Jessica asked him.

Drake paused a moment before answering. "Yes...." Silence quickly filled the area.

"I've never felt something for someone before," Drake finally said to break the silence. More silence then flooded the room. "Until I met you," he said very quietly.

"Me?" Jessica asked, a little shocked, "why me?"

"You are strong and tough, yet kind and gentle. You always know what to do or say in any situation and the more we hang out," he paused and grabbed Jessica's hands, "I get this feeling of like warmth inside and it only grows each time." He paused again to see her reaction but she didn't move a muscle. Silence started to creep in again until Jessica reached over and kissed Drake right on the lips. The two waited just a moment, lips to lips, to see what would happen next. Slowly the two started kissing and before they knew it they were making out. Suddenly, what seemed like fireworks going off, balls of extraordinary colors exploded around the two. This startled the two, causing them to stop. Once they did, so did the lights.

"What was that?" Jessica asked.

"That my child was a Cisra Telmak," Oshwaia stated as he appeared in the doorway to the balcony. "I really do apologize for coming in right now but I was passing by and sensed the Cisra Telmak. I've never seen it happen in my life and I honestly wanted to see it."

"What do you mean sensed the Cisra Telmak?" Drake asked, confused.

"Each Cisra Telmak gives off an aura, unique to the two who created it. Come, and I will show you more." Then, he turned around to leave the room. Intrigued, both Drake and Jessica followed Oshwaia. He led them to the temple's library and then went deep within the library. He stopped at a shelf, looked for a book, and then finally pulled one out. They all went to a table where Oshwaia flipped through the pages until he stopped on the section about the Cisra Telmak. Drake and Jessica started reading about how the very first Cisra Telmak ever recorded was just before the Great War. They also read about how each living soul has a specific aura, based on that soul's personality. When two auras mix together perfectly, they create what looks like balls of extraordinary colors exploding around the two. They continued to read more when suddenly *Bang* came from nowhere. *Bang* came another followed by another. It almost seemed like someone or something was knocking on the wall. Suddenly, it stopped. The three were really confused when out of nowhere, a section of the library's wall came crashing inwards almost like something crashed into it. The dirt and dust started to settle when Drake helped Jessica and Oshwaia up.

"What was that?" Jessica asked as she brushed off the dirt.

"I am not for...," Oshwaia started to say when from outside the temple came a black-looking hand, right inside where the wall caved in. It tried to grab Drake but grabbed Jessica instead. She started screaming as the hand pulled her towards the opening in the wall. Drake had barely grabbed her hands before he was holding onto the edge of the opening, trying so hard to not let her go. He got a quick glance of the thing that grabbed Jessica. The entire creature or beast was as black as night as tall as the temple was. It looked at Drake, eyes whiter than paper then just disappeared. When it disappeared, it dropped Jessica but luckily, with Drake still holding on, she didn't fall far at all. Drake's grip was starting to slip.

"Just hold on Jessica!" he shouted at her.

"Okay," she replied because she trusted him. He started to pull her up but their grip kept slipping. There was only one way Drake knew of that would save Jessica. With all of his strength, he swung her back up into the library but by doing so, it caused himself to fly off of the ledge. He let go so she would safely slide back into the temple and Drake fell. He fell right past both entrances to the temple and into the endless pit he went.

Chapter Eighteen:
Change In Friendships

"Where did he go?" Jessica asked Oshwaia, "What's down there? Is he okay? Will he be okay?" He walked up to her as she looked out of the hole in the wall.

"There there my child," Oshwaia spoke in a calming tone, "everything will be alright."

"Where did he go?"

"It looks like he fell to the lower part of the labyrinth."

"What's down there?" Jessica asked, a little nervous.

"That my child I do not know," he replied. The two then decided to put together a search party and go find him.

Drake slowly opened his eyes and carefully sat up. The back of his head started throbbing and when he touched it, it increased his pain. After letting the pain ease a bit, Drake got up to see where he was. He looked around, but had no idea where he was. Lit torches seemed to be scattered around another maze-like level. He started wandering around, trying to find a way out when something in the distance caught his attention. It almost looked like an eccu, but almost ghostlike. It looked at him, then walked into a wall and disappeared. Drake was intrigued yet very nervous. He was all alone after all. He started towards the wall where the eccu creature disappeared.

"Drake," came Queen Evë's voice from the same direction he was heading in, "Drake, come to me." He started walking faster but suddenly came to a complete stop when he spotted a muslu directly in front of him. He slowly bent down and touched it but his hand went right through it. This muslu was definitely dead, or at least that's what Drake thought. The creature paid no attention to him at all.

"Drake, come to me," Queen Evë's voice again. He stood back up and headed towards her voice. Before he knew it, he was standing in a large opening with a lake towards the center of the room. At the edge of the water sat Queen Evë with several ghost-like creatures around her; eccus, muslus, vemqurs, zerminiens, and even pretrigas and buutris. Drake slowly approached Queen Evë.

"They are simply lost souls, bound to walk the realm for all eternity," Queen Evë stated, "they are completely harmless."

"What do you mean by realm?" Drake asked as he sat beside her.

"Well, you know of the Realm of Light and the Realm of Darkness correct?" she replied.

"Yes."

"When Light and Darkness created this universe, they created the realms of Light, Darkness, and us; the Realm of the Universe." She paused a moment as she stroked a few creatures. "I come here when the Realm of Light gets too lonely."

"Why don't you come see me, Jessica, and the others?" Drake asked.

"I'm sorry but it's complicated," was all she could reply with. Suddenly, Queen Evë rose. "I'll be back soon," she stated then just disappeared. Drake instantly became nervous as the creatures started to swarm him.

As Jessica, Kim, Zack, Father Sage, and Oshwaia made their way down the temple, no one said a word. Even Oshwaia was concerned because he had never been below the temple.

"So where are we going again?" Kim asked to break the silence.

"Below the temple," Jessica answered her.

"What's down there?" she asked, directing the question towards Oshwaia. No one answered her. Silence fell around them again until Oshwaia finally broke it.

"I've only heard rumors of what lies beneath the temple. I have never needed to journey this far before." For the rest of the way down, no one spoke a word nor made a sound. They were finally approaching the bottom when suddenly, Kim froze right in her tracks.

"What's wro," Father Sage started to ask until he noticed it too. Somehow, a cooculu landed on Kim's left shoulder except it wasn't alive.

"Interesting," Oshwaia said, looking at the creature, "intriguing." He studied it for a moment.

"What exactly is it?" Kim asked, really wanting the creature gone.

"It appears to be a cooculu who has died but yet to have moved on," Oshwaia answered. He instantly became happily intrigued. "I've only heard of this place. I never imagined it truly being real," he stated.

"What?" Kim asked, very confused.

"What do you mean real?" Jessica asked.

Oshwaia took a deep breath and began to explain, "I've read stories about a place called Souls of the Departed."

"Souls of the Departed?" Kim accidentally interrupted.

"It's said that when creatures with pure souls die before their time their souls don't move on but instead walk among us as ghostlike creatures," Jessica answered, hoping to be right.

"That is correct, my child," Oshwaia answered.

"Do you think Drake is here as well?" Kim curiously asked.

"I would assume so, my child."

"Let's get going then!" she demanded and took off running. The cooculu flew away as the others followed Kim, who was now calling out for Drake.

Drake slowly opened his eyes only to find the creatures going about their own ways. Drake looked down towards his hands and noticed his Tërcerlin symbol was glowing. Then, it faded away.

What happened? Did he cause them to stop?
Whatever did happen, Drake still needed to find his
way back. He looked around and decided to take
the path around the lake.

At the bottom, Father Sage had caught up
to Kim who was still shouting for Drake.

"Kim! Stop shouting!" he said, trying to
calm her down, "we don't know what's down here,
so best we stay quiet."

"I agree," Oshwaia agreed.

"Same here," as did Jessica.

"Alright," Kim said, quieting down,
"alright." She paused a moment, "now what?"

"Hmmmm," Father Sage thought as he
looked around, "this way." He started towards a
doorway, followed by Jessica, Kim, Zack, and
Oshwaia took the rear. Father Sage was about to

walk through a doorway when a werzer soul appeared. It came through the wall and headed right towards Kim, causing her to scream.

After a couple of turns, Drake was now walking down a hallway when from in front of him came a scream.

"Kim?" Drake quietly said. Could it really be her? It had to have been, and the others had to have been with her. He took off running as quick as he could, taking another left turn followed by a right turn and then straight forward. Not really watching where he was going, Drake ran right into Jessica, causing the two to fall with him on top and her on bottom.

"Drake!" Kim shouted in excitement. "Thank goodness you're safe!" Drake's eyes locked with Jessica's and for a moment it seemed they were the only two people in the world as they were both remembering their first kiss from earlier. Kim's happiness was instantly crushed when she saw the person she really liked completely enthralled by someone else. Kim eagerly cleared her throat to bring them back to reality, they immediately jumped having forgotten everyone else was around and they helped each other up. "Oh Drake," Kim said as she hugged him, "I was so worried about you."

"Awe, well thank you Kim," Drake replied as he hugged her back. Then he thanked and hugged everyone who came to help rescue him.

"Can we get out of here? This place really creeps me out!" Kim asked.

"Yeah, let's go," Drake said and they all began their way back up.

After a little ways up, Jessica was chatting with Oshwaia so Kim decided it was the best time to tell Drake how she really felt about him.

"Hey Drake?" she asked as she caught up to him.

"Yeah? What's up Kim?" he responded.

"Do you like me?" she asked abruptly.

"Of course I do you're my best friend."

"No not like that. I mean *more* than a friend?"

"What do you mean? Like a sister or something?"

"No. Look Drake, I know you seem to have these new feelings for Jessica, but I was wondering if you might have some of those same feelings towards me?"

"Ooohh....," that really got Drake's attention. "Kim, I do like you a lot," he started off, "but I see you more as, like a best friend, or part of the family. Please don't be mad I don't know what I would do without you. But hey listen I know you'll find someone special soon. Someone who will feel the same way about you as you do them."

She kind of half smiled, "Yeah, sure." The two then hugged and moved onward.

"Oshwaia?" Drake asked as they continued to climb.

"Yes, my child?" he responded.

"That thing that attacked us, what was that?"

"I am not entirely sure," was all he could say. The rest of the way back up, no one said a word. Drake had so many questions left unanswered and yet, many more were flooding in. Once back at the temple, the group was exhausted from their adventure and decided to call it a night. It was just Drake and Jessica left. They kissed again, sealing their love and yet unknowingly sealing their fates together as well.

Chapter Nineteen:
Stage Nine

"Welcome! Welcome!" Oshwaia said and the crowd cheered and roared, "contestants, welcome to Stage Nine." The crowd quieted down to see what was going to happen in this stage. "Father Sage will explain the rules for this stage," Oshwaia said then the two switched places.

"For Stage Nine, the goal is to be one of the two finalists to not fall. On your way to the level, you'll be handed a scroll with your starting location and a palbaltrea," Father Sage explained, "once at your location and the stage begins, you'll take your palbaltrea and try to knock off the other contestants until only two remain." He paused a moment, "wait for the signal and best of luck." The crowd started cheering and roaring as the ten remaining contestants started their way to the stage's level.

"Good luck Drake!" Jessica said as she grabbed her scroll and palbaltrea.

"Hey, you too Jessica!" He replied then grabbed his, and headed for his location.

Once all ten contestants were in place, Stage Nine begun.

Instantly, two contestants were pushed off of their starting pillars by other contestant's palbaltreas. Instantly, Drake knew exactly how to play this stage. The contestant in front of him started swinging. Suddenly, the contestant behind him started swinging too. Jessica managed to knock one contestant off and was now battling another while Lance was hard at work dodging blows yet trying to throw them as well. The contestant in front started slipping, giving Drake the opportunity to swing. He swung his palbaltrea, knocking the contestant off. With that same swing, he swung it around to block a blow swung by the contestant behind him. The two battled it out a bit, but Drake was victorious by causing that contestant to fall as well. Drake looked around to see only four contestants remaining. Lance had moved pillars, and was heading towards Jessica. As Drake started off towards the two, Jessica managed to knock off the fourth contestant. One left to fall and that would end the stage.

By the time Drake had gotten over to the other two, they were really battling it out. Without hesitation, Drake started to attack Lance because he wanted to battle Jessica in the final stage. The two fought against Lance, but he didn't back down nor try to attack Drake. He just kept trying to attack Jessica. Soon, all three begin to grow tired. Jessica knew she was about beat. After deciding she wanted Drake to face Lance in the final stage, she looked up over at Drake. She smiled only enough for him to see then allowed Lance to knock her off, making it look like an accident. The moment Jessica fell, Stage Nine ended.

"First, let us give a round of applause to the ninety-eight contestants who participated in this year's Tessr Games," Oshwaia stated and the crowd cheered and roared, "and let us give a round of applause to our two finalists, Drake Shaw and Lance Jefferson." The crowd cheered and roared louder. After quieting the crowd, Oshwaia wrapped up Stage Nine. "That concludes Stage Nine. Stage Ten will commence in two days' time so go, rest, and best of luck.

Later that evening as Drake made his way from his home towards the temple, everyone he passed either congratulated him, wished him luck, or even both.

"Wow, you're more popular now than you were before," Zack was surprised at all of the attention Drake was getting.

"Yeah," was all he said.

"Drake, are you alright?" Zack asked, starting to become concerned.

"I.... I don't know but I can sense something is not right," Drake replied. The two headed to the temple to speak with Oshwaia.

"Oshwaia?" Drake called out as the two entered the temple, "Oshwaia, are you there?"

"Yes my child," he answered as he exited a room, "and I know why you are here."

"You do?" Zack asked surprisingly.

"Lord Taoî has found four of the six entrances," Oshwaia answered, "it is only a matter of time before."

"Lord Taoî gets through," Drake interrupted him.

"Correct," he replied. Drake instantly started tensing up.

"Drake, what's wrong?" Zack was very concerned, but so was Drake. He wasn't strong enough to defeat Lord Taoî and he needed more time but time was definitely not on his side.

Chapter Twenty:

Stage Ten

The day finally came, the tenth and final stage to this year's Tessr Games and Drake was just so surprised he had made it this far. Just before he awoke, Queen Evë called out to him.

"Darkness is coming," her voice echoed inside Drake's head, then came a vision. It started with the first entrance, the one they all used to escape Lord Taoî. *Boom* came a very large thumping noise. *Boom* it rang twice, then *Boom* again. Suddenly it stopped. For a moment, nothing happened. Then, out of nowhere an even louder *Boom* came and Darkness started flooding in. Drake's vision took him to the other entrances, where Darkness broke through each one and with the last entrance breached, in came Lord Taoî. The intenseness of the vision woke Drake right up. He looked around only to find he was still in his bed and everything looked normal but this really made Drake start to worry even more.

Drake and Zack got ready and then headed over to Jessica's home.

"Are you ready?" Jessica asked as she finished getting ready.

"No…. but yes," Drake replied after taking a deep breath.

"You've got this!" Jessica encouraged him.

"Yeah, I guess," Drake answered hesitantly. After Jessica was ready, the three met up with Kim and Prince Evergreen and the five headed to the temple for Drake's final preparation.

Once ready, Lance hurried to where he first met Lord Taoî. The moment he was there, he quickly summoned the Lord of Darkness.

"Yes, my numoni?" he asked.

"I am one of the finalists in this year's Tessr Games, my lord," he answered.

"And what is this Tessr Games?" Lord Taoî responded.

"It's an annual game held once a year. The victor of each game will train with the Last Archaic to prepare them to fight you and Darkness." Silence fell between the two until Lord Taoî started laughing.

"This is perfect!" he started to say, "You win this year's....games....and they will trust you completely."

"Then I can tell you every secret this Last Archaic has and you can finally rule all," Lance finished.

"You have impressed me," Lord Taoî was very pleased, but Lance did not look at all satisfied. "What is it?" Lord Taoî asked.

"Oh, nothing. Just I'm up against 'The Chosen One'," he replied. Tension quickly filled around the room.

"'THE Chosen One'?" Lord Taoî asked, showing just a little glimpse of fear.

"Yeah, Drake Shaw."

"Drake Shaw? Hmmmm," Lord Taoî paused, "step back." Lance did as he was told. The sphere then turned pitch black. Only but a few seconds passed and it began to change. It changed its shape and formed into a sword, with a blackened handle. On the handle, there was a blood red stone in the center and two small spikes at each end.

"What is this?" Lance asked as he approached the sword.

"This is the Rasîloo Sword. Kill Drake Shaw with this and his soul will fall into Darkness, forever." Lance quickly grabbed the sword, feeling its power surging through him. He started to laugh and Lord Taoî joined him. Drake had no idea what was coming his way.

"The Irrösa Sword and Nitrözi Shield? Are you sure?" Drake asked.

"Yes my child, they do belong to you," Oshwaia answered as he handed Drake the two. Drake took them and had Jessica put them on for him. Drake turned and faced the group. He took a deep breath.

"Let's do this," he stated, determined.

"Welcome! Welcome!" Oshwaia said, "Welcome to the final stage!" The crowd cheered and roared. After a few moments of excitement, Oshwaia quieted the crowd. "Let us meet this year's two finalists; Drake Shaw and Lance Jefferson." The crowd cheered and roared for their favorite finalist. The crowd settled down and Oshwaia continued, "The rules to Stage Ten is the same as the past finals. The finalist who completely disarms his opponent will be the winner. Head down to the northern part of the level and wait for the signal. Best of luck to you both." The crowd cheered and roared.

"Hey, good luck to you Lance," Drake said as he attempted to shake hands. Lance grabbed his hand and whispered to where only Drake could hear, "It is you who will need the good luck,

Drake." Letting go, he smirked and then headed to the level where the real fun was about to begin.

"Nice....sword Lance," Drake said as he examined Lance's sword.

"Thanks," was all he could say. Drake kept looking at it.

"Where did you get it?" Drake finally asked.

"Doesn't matter," Lance stated. *Bong* the first signal rang, and the two got ready. All Drake had to do was fully disarm Lance and he wins. *Bong* the second signal rang. Drake took a deep breath, waiting for the third and final signal; the starting bell. *Bong* went the signal and the stage began.

Lance came at Drake, swinging his sword at Drake. Drake, remembering his training, fought back. Fighting and blocking each other's moves, Drake and Lance seemed very equal in strength, agility, and discipline. Suddenly, wall sections started popping up out of nowhere. Catching the two off guard, a wall split the two. Just like that, the room became a maze that the two had to find each other.

✧ ✧ ✧ ✧ ✧ ✧ ✧ ✧ ✧ ✧ ✧ ✧

In the Tessr Games Arena, the crowd cheered and roared as everyone watched on an xhexlokit. Things were heating up and they had only begun, but Oshwaia sensed something was off about this battle........and about Lance.

✧ ✧ ✧ ✧ ✧ ✧ ✧ ✧ ✧ ✧ ✧ ✧

After what seemed like forever, the two did not find each other but a way out. Drake and Lance were now searching for each other throughout the level. Drake started down a series of long hallways as Lance made his way back to the level's entrance. He went around it and kept going, keeping his guard up. Drake came to a dead end and was forced to turn around. Lance made it to a four-way and just kept going forward. He briefly went on only to come to either a left or right turn. Without hesitation, he turned right and into a somewhat lit, large room. Drake made his way back and was about to go forward when Lance saw Drake at the entrance of the room.

"Found you!" he shouted at Drake then took off towards him. Drake quickly took off towards the right then left at the four-way. Unfortunately, Lance was right behind him. Drake ran into a room and without hesitation, quickly jumped onto a platform. He got to the end of it and instantly realized that the platform was over what looked like an endless pit. He immediately turned around only to watch Lance enter the room.

Kim was so nervous that she and Jessica were holding each other. Oshwaia was still worried. But what was about to happen next was going to throw everyone for a huge loop.

Just before Lance was about to jump onto the platform, it started to move away towards another platform across the pit. He quickly stopped, looked around the room, and then without any hesitation, darted for the other platform. He jumped onto it and the platform jolted forward towards Drake. Lance continued to the edge of his platform, sword ready to strike. Drake walked over to the edge of his platform and prepared for Lance's attack. The two platforms got close enough and Lance took a few steps back then ran and jumped towards Drake.

Drake quickly dodged Lance completely and prepared to strike Lance but before he even got a chance to strike, Lance jumped on top of him and knocked off Drake's shield. The Nitrözi Shield spun towards the edge of the platform and just like that, it fell into the pit below. Lance was about to swing when the two platforms collided with each other, causing Lance to become unbalanced. Drake shoved Lance off of him, quickly got up, and headed towards Lance. Just as Lance got up, Drake swung but Lance blocked with his shield. He swung his sword towards Drake, which forced Drake to jump back.

Lance continued to swing towards Drake and just like reflexes should, Drake blocked Lance's attack with his sword. At the same time, Drake did a high kick which knocked Lance's shield out of his hands and slid away. This angered Lance. He swung and swung at Drake, who just kept dodging them. Now, Lance was furious. An enormous strength spurt suddenly came to Lance and he swung at Drake but this time, Drake wasn't so lucky to dodge. Lance's sword cut Drake's left arm.

Jessica, Kim, and Oshwaia all stood up in shock. The crowd oohed and awed at the trick when in reality, NO ONE was supposed to get hurt. Oshwaia himself put a special spell on the level to prevent anyone from getting hurt but somehow, Lance found a way around it. Oshwaia quickly studied the sword Lance was wielding.

"The Rasîloo Sword," he whispered to himself and instantly knew that Drake was in real danger.

Pushing through the pain, Drake battled Lance sword verses sword. Another enormous strength spurt came to Lance, cutting Drake's right leg.

✧ ✧ ✧ ✧ ✧ ✧ ✧ ✧ ✧ ✧ ✧ ✧

The crowd began to cheer and roar a little as they continued to believe it was all just a trick. However, Jessica, Kim, and Oshwaia's worry only worsened.

✧ ✧ ✧ ✧ ✧ ✧ ✧ ✧ ✧ ✧ ✧ ✧

In so much pain, Drake looked into Lance's eyes and saw the darkness within. He instantly knew something wasn't right and he HAD to win. *Clang Clang* their swords struck each other, *Clang*

237

Clang Clang. It seemed liked it was forever swinging at each other. Sweat started dripping from both of their faces, but they were starting to tire out as well. A great opportunity arose as Lance started to slip and Drake quickly took it. With all his strength left, Drake swung his sword quicker than ever before. As it struck Lance's sword, not only did it force the sword out of his hand, the Rasîloo Sword split into two. The two pieces fell and slid over near Lance's shield.

"No!" Lance said angrily, knowing he had truly lost the games. They stood up and just stared at each other.

The crowd broke out with a sea of cheering and roaring. On the xhexlokit, Lance and Drake shook hands and Jessica and Kim sighed in relief. Drake had won the final stage and the fifth Tessr

Games. This had beyond angered both Lance and Lord Taoî himself.

Lord Taoî's anger was rising and rising until it took a complete one hundred and eighty turn when he had received some good news. He had just located the last two entrances. It was finally time to take his revenge as the attack on 'The Chosen One' and his followers was about to begin.

Chapter Twenty-One:
The Attack Begins

"I'm sorry, my lord," Lance said as he bowed.

"Rise my new ynerea. Even though you lost the games, the battle has only begun," Lord Taoî stated.

"Does that mean you found them?" Lance asked, a little excited.

"Indeed I have, but I will need your help to access them." Both Lord Taoî and Lance smiled at each other for they both knew what needed to be done. "Go to the Jewel City's entrance. You'll know what to do from there," Lord Taoî ordered Lance. He nodded in agreement and started to get ready for an attack he was yet hoping for.

After sneaking around both the living/housing level and the labyrinth of the Archaics, he made it to the entrance. Lance reached out and felt an extremely strong force field type spell. He had no magic, no special skills, nothing. How was he supposed to destroy this spell? He pulled out the Book of Megi and started shuffling through it. He read every chant and studied every spell but nothing seemed to help him. Lance was getting upset. He slammed his fists against the spell with frustration and something interesting happened. The spell weakened where he struck. Intrigued, he slammed his fists against the spell again and it weakened again but only in the spots where he was striking. He kept striking the spell until finally, both hands went through the spell. Very slowly and carefully, Lance forced his way through the spell. And just like that, he was on the other side of the spell. He looked around but it only seemed to have been a dead end. But why such a strong spell? Lance closed his eyes and concentrated. He needed to remember the day Lord Taoî and Darkness took over Jewel City.

He remembered following his mother and father with his little sister on his back into the library. He also remembered running towards a giant rounded stone wall and then down a rounded staircase until him and his family were safe in the Labyrinth of the Archaics.

"Stairs!" Lance said as he opened his eyes. He looked around for a rounded staircase but nothing. "Crazy old Oshwaia must have hidden it," he stated and then began searching for it. *Bang* Lance suddenly ran right into what seemed to have been an invisible wall. "Ugh," he snarled as he rubbed his face. He paused a moment then chanted, "Unsdao paque taraka." Suddenly the rounded staircase upward appeared. "Better," Lance stated and began his journey upwards.

As Drake rested, Queen Evë pulled Drake into the Realm of Light.

"Queen Evë? What's wrong? Is everything alright?" Drake asked as he began to worry.

"Yes dear, but take my hand," she replied. As he took her hand, the two suddenly flew. They journeyed through the living/housing level, part of the Temple, and into the labyrinth. They slowed down and came to a stop. The two landed and Drake let go.

"Now what?" he asked.

"Look," Queen Evë said as she pointed to the wall south of them. Drake studied the wall; nothing.

"I don't see anything out of the ordinary," Drake finally said.

"Look harder," Queen Evë said. Drake did as he was instructed. He looked harder and suddenly, he began to see through the wall. On the other side of the wall, it looked like there was a large room with four figures inside. Drake concentrated harder and identified the figures as four hiumäns, one being Father Izea, another man Drake did not recognize, and....his parents! The shock of seeing his parents again instantly woke Drake up and sprung him forward, waking and startling Zack.

"Drake, what's wrong?" Zack asked him.

"My parents," was all he could say as he put his shoes on. He then darted out of his home with Zack right behind. The two were headed towards the level's entrance when he first ran into Kim.

"Drake? What's going on? Is everything alright?" Kim asked him as he approached.

"My parents!" he shouted as he ran past her.

"Drake's parents?!" she asked and took off towards them. As they got to the level's entrance, Drake, Kim, and Zack almost zoomed past Jessica as they headed upwards.

"Whoa, what's going on?" Jessica exclaimed as everyone kind of surprised her.

"I'm not sure, but it has something to do with Drake's parents!" Kim explained, "Come on!"

The four reached the labyrinth. Nobody said a word as they followed Drake into the maze. After several left and right turns, Drake finally stopped.

He stared at the wall itself. The other three did the same. They all stood there in pure silence for what seemed like hours until they all heard very faint knocking from beyond the wall they were staring at.

"I knew it!" Drake finally spoke.

"Knew what?" Jessica asked.

"I was resting a while ago," Drake began to explain it all, "When Queen Evë came to me. She showed me that beyond the wall," he pointed at the wall, "there is a room and my parents are trapped inside."

"Quick Zack, go get Oshwaia!" Jessica said and Kim agreed.

"Right away!" Zack said excitedly as he turned into a dailooo and just like that, he was gone.

The three only waited a short time before the two showed up. Drake explained to Oshwaia about the situation and he instantly agreed to help him out.

"I can change and manipulate the walls to connect the room with this hallway but it will only be for a brief time so you must hurry," Oshwaia said.

"I understand," Drake agreed.

"Are you ready?" Oshwaia asked. Zack turned back into a silver wolf as Drake walked up to him.

"Ready!" Drake answered. Oshwaia stuck his hands out and started twisting and turning them. Shortly afterwards, the wall in front of them all began to change.

"It just won't budge," Father Izea stated as he tried to open the giant door again. Doreen started to cry for she was scared and not knowing if they'll make it out alive. The others began to start to think the same way. Doreen stopped crying when she suddenly heard cracking noises coming from the wall the giant door was attached to.

"What was that?" Andrew started to say until the wall itself started to change. It changed and manipulated, creating one room with a hallway attached.

"Mom! Dad!" Doreen and Steve suddenly heard Drake's voice from within the hallway. "Mom! Dad!" it came again, "please hurry towards my voice." Without any hesitation, the four grouped together and hurried towards Drake's voice.

As the two walls merged together, Drake quickly started calling out to his parents. They all waited for a response, but heard nothing. He called to them again, but still no response.

"I cannot hold this for much longer child," Oshwaia finally said, which instantly worried Drake. What happens if they can't hear him? He was this close to getting his parents back after five years of being captive. Just as Oshwaia was about to stop, Kim saw something coming towards them.

"Look!" she shouted and pointed at figures running their way. It was Drake's parents. Oshwaia pushed to hold on a little longer as the four broke through the manipulated wall and into the hallway. Once the four safely made it through, Oshwaia ended the manipulation and things went back to normal.

"Mom! Dad!" Drake shouted as he ran to them.

"Son!" they exclaimed as the three of them hugged each other for the longest time. Lord Taoî had Drake's parents held captive for over five years now and they were finally free at last.

"I have so much to tell you," Drake said as they all pulled away.

"As do we son," Steven said then the entire group started laughing.

Lord Taoî, Michael Cashner, and some oxxtrades waited until the Tërcerlin symbol on the ground started to glow. Then, the ground started to shake and the glowing Tërcerlin symbol rose clockwise. Shortly afterwards it stopped, revealing a spiral staircase leading downward. From below emerged Lance Jefferson. As he reached the top of the staircase, the oxxtrades darted towards him and the stairs.

"Stop!" he ordered and just like that, they all stopped dead in their tracks. Lord Taoî's face went from pleased to see Lance to interest that he was another being who could control Pure Darkness. "I myself made it through Oshwaia's spell but it is still up," Lance explained.

"It's alright my ynerea," Lord Taoî started to say.

"Why call me your ynerea?" Lance quickly asked.

"Why, because I see much darkness in you and I'd like you to rule Pure Darkness by my side," Lord Taoî answered him.

"And rule Pure Darkness by your side I shall," Lance responded as the approached the Master of Darkness himself. They shook hands and began laughing. "Now shall we begin?" Lance asked after they stopped laughing. Lord Taoî smiled and Pure Darkness appeared only around Lord Taoî and Lance. Michael seemed to have been "kicked out" of the group. Then, Lord Taoî and

Lance rose high into the sky. They came to a stop high in the clouds.

"Attack!" Lord Taoî shouted into the wind above. His one word echoed across the entire planet, and at that exact moment, all six entrances became under attack.

Drake stopped dead in his tracks.

"Drake, are you okay?" Doreen stopped and asked. Drake did not answer. He just stared forward.

"Drake?" Jessica asked as the rest of the group stopped as well.

"It has begun," he very quietly said. *Bang,* came a large sound from somewhere within the labyrinth. *Bang, Bang…. Bang, Bang, Bang…. Bang, Bang, Bang, Bang….* it sounded like several different points throughout the labyrinth were

being battered. *Bang, Bang, Bang, Bang, Bang*....
Bang, Bang, Bang, Bang, Bang, Bang.... *Bang,*
Bang, Bang, Bang, Bang, Bang.... *Bang, Bang,*
Bang, Bang, Bang, Bang.... it seemed to be six
places being banged on........ the six entrances.

After everyone made it safely back to the
temple, Oshwaia and Drake together created a new
force field like spell around the temple itself. On
the way down to the living/housing level, Oshwaia
put up more spells for more protection.

"Everyone," Drake said to get the groups
attention, "somehow, Lord Taoî found the
labyrinth entrances. Soon, he will make his way
into here and we need to be ready but do not tell
ANYONE! We cannot have panic!" Everyone
nodded in agreeament. "Oshwaia?" he turned
towards the last archaic, "Please go gather the

other four victors and bring them back here."
Without saying a word, Oshwaia headed off for the
first victor. "Jessica and Kim?" he asked the two,
"please take my parents and, umm," he didn't
know Andrew's name yet.

"Andrew Lee sir," Andrew introduced
himself.

"And Andrew to get looked at."

"But Drake?" his mother started to say.

"I will be fine, I promise. We will meet up
later on," he assured her.

"Alright," she said and the five were off.

"And you Father Izea," he turned and
looked him dead in the eyes, "come with me."
Then took off. Father Izea gulped with concern and
followed with Zack in the rear. The two followed
Drake to Father Izea's home.

"Take me to your hidden room please,"
Drake asked him.

"How....how do you know about that room?!" he demanded to know.

"Father Izea, please just take me there. We don't have much time," Drake responded.

"Alright alright," Father Izea gave in. Zack looked over Lance's house across the way and noticed his front door was standing wide open.

"Hey Drake? I'll be right back. I need to check on something real quick," Zack told Drake.

"Alright, just be careful," Drake replied. And with that, Drake and Father Izea went into the home while Zack headed over to Lance's Zack slowly creeping up to the open door. He stood there for a moment, wondering what to do. After much thought, Zack very slowly and very carefully entered the house.

While searching the home, there was no sign of Lance, anywhere. This started to concern Zack as he got a bad feeling. As he exited the house, he noticed Jane Florence headed straight towards him.

"Hey Zack," she said, "is Lance home by any chance?"

"Strangely, no," he answered.

"Now I'm definitely suspicious!" she stated. This confused Zack.

"Suspicious? Suspicious of what?" he asked.

"I saw Lance sneaking around here a while ago and as I went to follow him, he just vanished."

"Vanished?!"

"Yeah, I can't find him anywhere so I thought I would just check his house."

"Oh, I see. His door was standing wide open so I went to investigate but there's no sign of him here," Zack said.

"I have a bad feeling about this," Jane was really beginning to worry when Zack had an idea.

"Hey, come with me and let's go tell Drake this. He's just next door," Zack said to try to ease her some.

"That's a good idea Zack. Let's go," she said and then the two headed off next door.

"Look, about me running off before," Father Izea started to say as they made their way to his hidden room, "....can you forgive me?"

"Try your hardest to answer what I am about to ask of you then yes," Drake replied. They finished their walk in silence and entered the hidden room. They walked up to Father Izea's working table. Drake pulled out the Calzaniti Statue.

"How quickly can you create a duplicate of this?" Drake asked as he gently tossed the statue to Father Izea.

He caught it, inspected it for a moment and said, "Two, maybe three hours tops."

"I need a duplicate right away please," Drake asked Father Izea, who nodded in agreeance and immediately went to work. Drake then began to leave.

"Drake?" Father Izea stopped him just before he walked out.

"Yes?" he replied as he turned towards Father Izea.

"Thank you," Father Izea said softly. Drake nodded and exited the room.

As he left Father Izea's home, Jane Florence and Zack came running up to him. They explained to him what happened. Drake instantly became just as worried as the other two.

"Go see if he is in the Training Room and then report back to Oshwaia's home," he kindly asked.

"Sure," Jane and Zack said and headed off as Drake headed towards Oshwaia's.

Once the last victor was present, Drake begun to explain exactly what was going on.

"Excuse me? Your attention please," Drake asked kindly as he got the four's attention, "We have a very drastic situation on our hands."

"Like what?" Ryan McNalley interrupted.

"Someone can't get a date?" Jared Olson teased. Both he and Ryan started laughing.

"It is time," Oshwaia started up, "this is the moment you all have been training with me for." Immediately, the two stopped laughing and all four victors went cold.

"Lord Taoî has found all six entrances to the labyrinth and soon he will break in, along with Darkness itself," Drake started speaking, "Oshwaia and I have tried to prevent this from happening but there is no stopping it." He paused a moment to let the information sink in. "You four need to report to the level's entrance. There, do whatever it takes to stop Lord Taoî and Darkness from entering." The four agreed.

"Do we have much time?" Ryan asked.

"No," Drake said.

"How, how long do we really have?" Tori Eckerburg asked with worry in her voice. Drake did not answer but instead, silence filled the room. Finally, Drake took a deep breath and spoke.

"Hours" he stated, "….if that."

Chapter Twenty-Two:
Closing Ceremony

The day of the Closing Ceremony had finally come and Drake had never been more on edge. Security was tripled but he still had a bad feeling.

"Drake?" Jessica asked, "Are you okay?"

"You know, I don't know. No one has seen Lane since he lost and I have a very bad feeling about his disappearance," he answered.

"I have the same feeling," she replied as she got up and headed towards the door. "Do you think what we saw will happen?" she nervously asked.

"I hope not," he stated, "for everyone's sake." He got up and the two together headed towards the Tessr Games Arena.

"Welcome! Welcome!" Oshwaia said as the crowd cheered and roared. Shortly afterwards, they calmed down and Oshwaia started the ceremony. "Welcome to the Closing Ceremony of the fifth annual Tessr Games. I would first like to thank every contestant who participated this year." The crowd cheered and roared as each contestant rose to be recognized, including Jessica. The crowd quieted down as the contestants sat back down. "Now, let us welcome the victor of this year's Tessr Games," Oshwaia announced. Instantly, the crowd cheered and roared like crazy. "Drake Shaw!" Oshwaia pointed as Drake himself walked in. The crowd continued to cheer and roar. As Drake walked towards Oshwaia to accept the Calzaniti Statue, Jessica instantly remembered when she first saw it. Drake walked all the way up to Oshwaia and just as Drake was about to receive the Calzaniti Statue, a large *Bang* came from above the arena. *Bang* came another. Suddenly, *BANG* came the largest ever. Without even getting the opportunity to respond, Darkness came through the entrance of the arena, followed by Lord Taoî himself.

"Drake!" Jessica shouted then started running towards him as chaos started breaking out all over the arena. As Lord Taoî approached Drake, he quickly pulled out the real Calzaniti Statue. This actually surprised Lord Taoî. Drake held out the statue towards Lord Taoî who instantly started to disappear into the statue itself. Things seemed to have been going well when Lance Jefferson appeared chanting a spell from the Book Of Megi. Jessica reached the ground but couldn't make out what Lance was chanting. Lance finished chanting and immediately closed the book. Suddenly, a bright light appeared around Drake, nearly blinding almost everyone in the room and causing Drake to drop the statue.

"Drake, no!" Jessica shouted as the light grew. Then, it dissipated. She quickly looked around to see everything was exactly the way it was before the light except for one thing; Drake had disappeared. Lord Taoî and Lance both laughed as Darkness finally took over the last of Light, but what exactly happened to Drake was all Jessica could think about, as well as the rest of his friends and family....

To be continued....